I,
EMMA
FREKE

I, EMMA FREKE

Elizabeth Atkinson

CAROLRHODA BOOKS · Minneapolis

Carolrhoda Books
A division of Lerner Publishing Group, Inc.
241 First Avenue North
Minneapolis, MN 55401 U.S.A.

Website address: www.lernerbooks.com

Cover art: © Rammal Mehmud

Interior photos: (feathers) © iStockphoto.com/Alexander Potapov, half title page; (clouds) © iStockphoto.com/Aleksejs Polakovs, half title page, title page, 1, 6, 17, 24, 32, 37, 44, 50, 56, 63, 72, 79, 86, 96, 103, 113, 125, 138, 147, 155, 161, 168, 176, 181, 191, 199, 208, 217, 224; (grass) © iStockphoto.com/Nadezda Firsova, title page.

Library of Congress Cataloging-in-Publication Data

Atkinson, Elizabeth.
    I, Emma Freke / by Elizabeth Atkinson.
       p.   cm.
    Summary: Growing up near Boston with her free-spirited mother and old-world grandfather, twelve-year-old Emma has always felt out of place, but when she attends the family reunion her father's family holds annually in Wisconsin, she is in for some surprises.
    ISBN: 978-0-7613-5604-2 (trade hard cover : alk. paper)
    [1. Eccentrics and eccentricities—Fiction. 2. Family reunions—Fiction.
3. Single-parent families—Fiction. 4. Family life—Massachusetts—Fiction.
5. Family life—Wisconsin—Fiction. 6. Massachusetts—Fiction. 7. Wisconsin—Fiction.] I. Title.
PZ7.A86373Iae 2010
[Fic]—dc22   2009038923

Manufactured in the United States of America
3 – SB – 12/31/11

With love and appreciation
for my original freaky family!
Mom, Dad, Peter,
Jennifer (& Raven)

And in memory of
my old black lab, China,
my writing companion
for thirteen years

ONE

"Let's say you were the hands on a clock with the least popular time being one o'clock all the way up to the most popular time being twelve o'clock. What time would *you* be?"

The school psychologist, Ms. Fiddle, studied me as if I were an experiment about to bubble over.

"Do you mean what's my favorite time of the day?"

Ms. Fiddle shifted in her big cushy office chair and stared down at her binder.

"Let's do this a different way," she said in a fake, perky voice. "Look at the clock on the wall behind me."

It was a flat white clock with two pencils telling the time.

"Now, *who* would you say is the most popular girl in your grade?"

I had to think about that one as there were lots of incredibly popular girls in the sixth grade.

"Um. I guess it's a tie between Savannah Lipton and Akira Washington."

Ms. Fiddle rolled her eyes.

"Just pick one."

"The very most popular one?"

"*Any*one," she said sharply.

"Should I still look at the clock?"

"No, *yes*—wait," she groaned. "Okay. Let's try this one more time."

Ms. Fiddle forced herself to speak in a really calm voice, but it was too calm, sort of like the pause just before lightning strikes the ground and explodes.

"If Savannah Lipton, let's say, represented a time on the popularity clock, what time would she be?"

I glanced up at the wall and said very carefully, "Twelve o'clock?"

"That's right!" she hollered like a game show host. "I mean, good."

Then she rolled her chair so close to me our knees practically touched.

"So if Savannah is twelve o'clock, the most popular hour, what time are *you*?"

At that very moment a fly buzzed across the room and landed on Ms. Fiddle's shoulder. I could tell she knew it was there, but she ignored it and stared right into my eyes.

"Um. One minute past twelve?" I said in a tiny voice, because I wasn't sure if there was a correct answer or if she really had no idea how invisible I was in middle school.

Without turning her head she reached across her collarbone and smacked the fly dead, then flicked it off her shoulder.

"We were not including minutes," said Ms. Fiddle, arching one eyebrow so high it made that side of her mouth droop. "Just *hours*."

But before I could correct my answer, Ms. Fiddle whipped her chair around and began typing on her computer. I sat silently and waited for directions. I never knew where she was going next with these sessions.

Suddenly, she stopped to look back at me over her slit glasses.

"You may go to your next class now, Emma. We'll meet again on Thursday from 10:35 until 11:21."

She returned to her typing as if she had a deadline in about six seconds.

"Excuse me, Ms. Fiddle?"

"Hmm?" she replied without missing a letter on her keyboard.

"Do the minutes count on Thursday, or should I come from ten o'clock to eleven o'clock?"

Not five minutes later, I was ducking behind a dumpster out in the school parking lot. I waited there until I heard the indoor bell signaling the next class. I knew the halls would be flooded soon, and no one would bother to look out a window at someone escaping across the pavement and into the woods.

I did this twice a week whenever I had a session with Ms. Fiddle. All my teachers knew I went to the school psychologist for "socialization skills," so on my session days, they all basically lost track of me. Or at least, they figured I wasn't their responsibility. And Ms. Fiddle never checked to see if I actually returned to class. She just flicked me away like that dead fly.

It was the same on my walk home. No one ever stopped to ask me why I wasn't in school as I strolled down the sidewalk along Harbor Street. It may have been because I was invisible in the outside world too. But I think it had more to do with the fact that I was five feet ten inches tall, almost six feet if I stood up straight (which I never did). So I guess everyone assumed I was basically grown up, even though I was just turning twelve in five days.

The reason I ignored kids my age and they ignored me was pretty simple. I just didn't fit in. Not with the geeks, the emos, the gossipers, the preps, or even the losers. To them I didn't exist. Even the teachers seemed to avoid me. And Ms. Fiddle was only interested in studying me like a misplaced giraffe caged with a pack of hyenas.

Life wasn't always like this. In fact, when I was younger and shorter and dumber, I usually had one or two friends to play with at recess. My grades were good but nothing special. Then my height and brains took off one summer as if someone watered me with too much fertilizer. Even my dull hair turned redder.

To make matters worse—to make matters *impossibly* worse—my name is Emma Freke.

Like, if you say it slowly, *Am a Freak*.

For some reason, my mother, Donatella, chose my name without saying it out loud. And I never could figure out if my weird name made me more of a freak or if I would have been a mega-freak anyway.

T W O

As I rounded the corner of Driftwood Lane, I saw the Closed sign in our store window. Donatella must have overslept. I checked my watch. If I hadn't ditched school, I would be sitting down to an early lunch. Alone, of course.

We owned a little shop, Freke Beads & More, and lived on the second floor just above the giant sign. As if having the last name Freke wasn't bad enough, my mother decided to plaster it across the one place where we spent most of our waking *and* sleeping hours.

She had taken over the building a long time ago from my grandfather, Lorenzo Salvoni, who had used the same space to sell his homemade Italian pastas and meals for more than forty years. He still lived with Donatella and me but had nothing to do with the beads. I don't think he even understood why people would buy beads. And the

"More" part of our business was pretty vague to me as well. Donatella claimed she specialized in whatever made people feel *centered*. That included almost anything from tea leaf readings to foot massages.

But I have to admit, I loved our store. I loved it more than anything else in my life.

The shop was a maze of counters lined with wooden boxes containing millions of beads. Some were as shiny and plump as bright-colored berries. Others were carved from wood, like the Brazilian patterned nut bead, rough with brown dots. All the beads were arranged in such an orderly fashion, not one out of place unless a customer accidentally mixed it up. In fact, it was my primary responsibility every day to make sure the beads were all in their correct cubbies. And that's where they stayed until they were bought and arranged on a necklace or earrings or a bracelet. But even then, the beads knew where they belonged, in a neat and pretty pattern. Individually they were all special, and when combined, they were even more amazing. No matter what they looked like, beads knew how to socialize perfectly.

As I stood in front of the store, I stared at my reflection in the glass. Yep, I was pretty hideous. Everything about me drooped—my eyes, my mouth, even my ears. No wonder no one at school liked me. I didn't even like me.

I took out my key ring and unlocked the door. A rush of cold, musty air washed over the sidewalk. So as soon as I turned on the lights, I powered up the space heater.

Even though it was late May, it was still a bit chilly outside. We lived less than a mile from the Atlantic Ocean, so the coastal breeze was often cool and salty. But lately, the skies had been windier than usual.

Once inside, I switched on the twangy Indian music, lit the incense, and changed the sign to OPEN.

"Emma-roni! You home?"

My grandfather, Nonno, called out my name as he came down the back stairs from our apartment to the bead shop. He seemed to have no idea when I was supposed to be in school but was always relieved when I arrived home. His old bulldog, Eggplant Parmigiana (named after his customers' all-time favorite menu item), struggled down the narrow steps behind him. The round dog was dirty white with a half-black, half-pink nose and a stump for a tail. Her jowls practically touched the ground, and she constantly snorted in and out, especially when she slept.

The two of them stopped at the bottom of the tiny stairway.

"Watch Eggplant! I get coffee at Pete's."

"Why don't you take her with you, Nonno?"

I glanced back at the old dog who had plopped down at my grandfather's feet, already asleep.

"Pete's cat no good," he said in his raspy voice, lifting his cane. "*Terrible* cat!"

I carefully picked three mint green seed beads out of a pile of striped glass beads and gently dropped them into the correct cubby.

"Okay, but she can't just lie there blocking the stairs."

My grandfather gave Eggplant some commands in Italian. She instantly lifted up her tired, pudgy body and waddled over to a spot under the cash register.

"Little sausage for the lunch?"

I sighed. We went through this all the time. Nonno would ask if I wanted him to get some food for me, but really he was just figuring out what he wanted to eat.

"Sure."

"And the rigatoni?"

"Whatever."

"Better the ziti?"

"Anything, Nonno, it all sounds fine."

My grandfather limped carefully through the cramped store. He stopped a minute to pull his brown beret out of his coat pocket and stretch it over his fuzzy white hair.

"Ciao, ladies!"

As he shuffled through the front door, Nonno hooked the handle with his cane and yanked it shut. A chain of gypsy bells hanging on the back of the door jingled loudly. Then the only sound in the store came from underneath the cash register. The motor of a very old dog, snorting in, snorting out.

I plucked five beads (two ovals and three marbled) from the bottom of a box of silver clasps.

"Donut Delivery!"

It was Penelope from across the street who was basically my best friend, since she was my only friend these days. Except it felt weird to admit it because Penelope was a little more than two years younger and fifteen inches shorter than me. She was in the fourth grade at the local Montessori school.

"Why are you home?" I asked her as I plucked ten misplaced earring wires from the Chinese twine tray.

"Half day for us! Parent-teacher conferences."

Penelope jumped up on the counter next to the cash register and threw a piece of a jelly donut hole down to Eggplant.

"No more please. She already poops enough."

I trailed my hand through a cubby of smooth shell beads, feeling for anything that didn't belong.

"So why are *you* home?" she asked. "Ms. Fiddly-Diddly messing with your mind today at school?"

I brushed off my hands and chose a plain donut from the box.

"Yep, and I guess it's a good thing. Looks like Donatella had a late date last night. The shop was closed when I got here."

Donatella was not your typical mother who ever went by Mommy or Mom or even Ma. She felt it categorized her, like one of the beads. To everyone in the world, including her only daughter, she was just *Donatella*.

And that meant, she didn't have to act like a mother either.

"Who's she going out with now?" Penelope mumbled, her mouth full of pastry.

I went behind the counter to check the cash drawer. No money other than a few nickels and pennies placed in the wrong slots.

"Larry or Gary or some name like that."

Donatella was forty-seven years old and had been married and divorced two and a half times before she turned thirty-four. (The half being her first marriage when she was a teenager; Nonno had it annulled.) From then on, she vowed never to walk down the aisle again. But she continued to date men with the passion of a high school cheerleader.

Somehow in all those marriages and relationships she had only given birth once, to me. And even more unbelievable, she kept the last name of her most recent husband, Walter Freke. She claimed it was memorable, a good business choice. And Walter Freke? According to Donatella, he "bolted like a branded steer" a full year before I was born. I wasn't even related to the guy, and yet, I was forced to advertise his horrible name like one of those enormous billboards on Route 1. While my real father remained a mystery.

The strange part was I looked nothing like my mother. In fact, we were the exact opposite of one another. Donatella was just barely five feet with curly black hair, hazel eyes, and golden olive skin. She was almost as wide and curvy as she was tall. She spent at least an hour every morning getting ready between choosing her jewelry and plastering on makeup.

Aside from being more than a head taller than my mother and half as ample, my skin was as white as one of the pearl beads. Except for the cinnamon freckles sprinkled across my face and down my arms. And my blue eyes were so faded, Nonno said they were the color of the ancient northern sky. I wore my bright red hair in a small bun at all times, so it would be less noticeable. And I didn't care at all about clothes or accessories.

Even though our lack of physical similarities was obvious, in my mind, what made us most different was our laugh. When Donatella laughed, she made everyone in the room stop and laugh too. And I never even let myself laugh in front of other people.

"So are both Gray Moms going to the parent-teacher conference?" I asked Penelope.

"Just Cynthia. Katherine's in Hong Kong again."

I often thought that Penelope was the one who should feel most like a freak, but she was probably the happiest, friendliest person I ever knew.

When Penelope was a baby, our neighbors, Cynthia and Katherine Windsor-Farthington, adopted her from Liberia. According to Penelope, they flew to Africa three times before they found the exact right infant meant just for them. And Penelope called them Gray Moms because they both had gray hair and looked more like grandmothers than mothers.

"Katherine's upset about missing the conferences," continued Penelope, "so Cynthia is going to call her on the cell phone before she meets with each teacher and then put her on 'speaker' so she can hear everything."

"All the way from Hong Kong?"

"Yep." Penelope searched through the box for another donut. "It's even going to be the middle of the night over there."

Penelope's Gray Moms loved her more than any other parents I knew. Even though they were super rich, it wasn't just that they gave her lots of stuff. It was more that they made Penelope feel as if she could do anything and they would be right there cheering her on. The three of them ate breakfast and dinner together every day when Katherine wasn't traveling for work. Penelope always had clean clothes neatly folded in her drawers, and she never once got left at the dentist office for three hours and forty-nine minutes.

Just then a customer walked into the store followed by a gust of cold air. He was very tall and very bald, and he wore a black suit that made him look like a banker or a lawyer. Penelope jumped off the counter and grabbed her box of pastries.

"Hi!" she chirped to the man. "Wanna donut?"

The man looked surprised, then grinned.

"No, thank you."

She whispered to me, "You want me to stay and help?"

"Nah, I'll call you later."

The man nodded at Penelope as she slipped out the front door. The long chain of bells jingled after she pulled it shut. I noticed the twangy Indian music had finished so I chose another CD called *Jungle Birds Awakening*.

I watched the man as he awkwardly peered into each square compartment. It was clear he had never been in a bead shop before, because he made a confused expression with every new item he discovered.

Even though I could barely speak to people my own age, particularly at school, I never had a problem chatting with our customers. I don't know why, but I always knew exactly what to say when I worked at the shop.

"Um. Are you looking for something in particular?" I asked the man as he stared intently at the collection of silk ribbons.

He pondered the question as if he had no idea what he wanted.

"I'm just looking," he finally replied.

"We have a special on Durango Chip beads," I suggested.

He turned and smiled.

"Actually, I'm not shopping at all. But—but thank you," he stammered, then left.

That was strange, I thought to myself. He seemed kinda flustered. All at once, I wondered if he was some official guy, like a collections officer or a banker checking us out. I wouldn't be surprised one bit if my mother forgot to pay her taxes.

Then the door shot open again. I knew right away this customer was one of Donatella's friends. He was wearing slick coveralls so he had to be a fisherman from the docks. The way he peered around the store, you'd think he stumbled into the underwear section at the department store.

"Uhhh," he said as he took off his cap. "I was looking for the lady who owns this place?"

I knew it. A fishy aroma washed over the shop.

"She's not here, but if you want, I can take a—"

At that moment, Donatella burst through the door, practically slamming the chain of bells against the wall.

"Kevin!!" she shouted and laughed at the same time.

The man instantly roared with laughter too.

"'Tella baby!! You're lookin' gorgeous," he grinned through a mouthful of crooked teeth. "Hey, your store is swell."

She shooed away the compliment and replied, "It pays the bills."

'Tella baby? Yuck.

"So!" he said rubbing his hands together as if he were starving to death. "Ready for a little lunch?"

My mother was wearing one of her prized sparkly skirts and a tight sweater covered in metallic discs. It looked like something a retired belly dancer would wear. I was surprised to see her up and out of bed and in full date mode. She usually went out with her men friends at night.

"Never been readier!" she squealed, giggling like a little girl.

I coughed my way into the conversation to get her attention.

"Ahem!"

"Oh here, Emma," she said without even glancing at me as she pulled an envelope out of her purse. Her other hand was gripping one of Kevin's suspenders as they stared all goofy at each other. "I tootled over to the bank to get cash for the drawer."

"Good, we were out."

As I divided the bills by value and cracked open the rolls of change, Donatella muttered something very strange to the man.

"It's not easy to get decent help these days—"

But before I could remind her that I was more than "the help," she tore her gaze away from him and asked, "Would you mind watching the shop, Emma? Kevin and I will be back in an hour or so."

What was she talking about? I was almost always watching the shop.

"Unless we find something better to do," Kevin growled, winking at both of us.

Ugh. Who was this guy?

I watched the two of them rush down the street, arm in arm, Donatella's skirt blowing so high you could see the top of her chunky legs. She didn't even care that I was supposed to be at school.

All of a sudden, I smelled something horrible. It was the dog trying to digest the donut hole.

"Gross, Eggplant!"

My whole life is a freak show, I thought to myself and sighed. No one had it as bad as I did.

T H R E E

"Happy Birthday DEAR EMMMMAAA . . . happy birthday to you!"

A few days later, Donatella, Penelope, Nonno, Eggplant, and I sat around the dinner table upstairs in our apartment, which was pretty cramped like the bead store. It consisted of one open space (which we called the Big Room) with two little bedrooms, a bathroom, and a loft upstairs in the attic where Nonno and Eggplant slept. The Big Room had a kitchen on one side and a sitting area on the other half where we mostly watched TV.

I was impressed that my mother had remembered my twelfth birthday and even bought a cake. It was a factory cake that came in a box from the grocery story in the frozen food aisle, but still.

I blew out the candles.

"Did you make a wish?" my mother beamed. She was the kind of person who believed in wishes.

"Maybe you wish stop the growing!" yelled Nonno and then laughed so hard he started to hack.

"If it were *me*," said Penelope, "I'd wish for an orange convertible Mustang GT with a chrome grille and spinner hubcaps . . . *or* a sister."

"A sister?" screeched Donatella. "Dear celestial heavens above, don't even joke about that."

Penelope, who was just as feisty as Donatella, straightened in her seat like a peacock spreading massive feathers.

"It's no joke! That's exactly what I'm asking the Gray Moms for when I turn ten in August. They said that since it's my big double-digit birthday, I can have *whatever* I ask for."

I frowned. Here I was thankful for a half-frozen strawberry cake from Shop & Stock while my only friend could have anything she wanted for her birthday. Maybe *I* could be Penelope's new sister.

"Hurry to cut cake, already," said Nonno who was starting to nod off a little.

Donatella tapped my hand as I picked up the knife.

"You didn't tell us what you wished for, Emma."

What I wished for? Where would I start? I wished for a normal mother who acted like one. I wished for a real house. I wished for friends. I wished to be shorter, prettier, funnier . . . all impossible wishes.

I looked at Donatella and wondered why she asked me that. She never cared about my dreams. She only cared about herself and who her next date would be.

"I forgot to make one," I said.

I wasn't the kind of person who believed in wishes.

"Well I bet there's one you *would* have wished for above all others, and I'm going to make it come true!"

My mother twirled around and ran over to the sofa under which she was hiding a box. Her flowing pink dress and colorful head scarf made her look a little like a fairy godmother.

"I give gift too," said Nonno. "*Mio* first!"

"No, me!" said Penelope who sprung out of her chair and dug into her pocket.

"Fine," said Donatella as she sat back down with a medium square box in her lap wrapped in violet paper and white ribbons. "Penelope, then Nonno, then me."

"Wow, I've never gotten this many presents before."

Getting a present was hit or miss in our house. My mother usually gave me some sort of IOU. Nonno would give me something he thought up in his head seconds before, like a stroll on the beach or sharing a box of popcorn. But ever since I had known Penelope, since she was one, she always gave me something really nice.

I opened her tiny pocket present. It was wrapped tightly in a little red paper bag with funny Asian letters printed on it.

"Oh my gosh, it's a gold bead."

Penelope stood up totally excited about her gift.

"It's a lot more than that—it's a good *mojo* gold bead!"

"What's good mojo?"

"You know, it's like a magic charm that brings good luck!"

Donatella shoved on her striped reading glasses and studied it.

"Where'd you find that? Maybe we can get those for the store."

"Katherine got it for me in Hong Kong. I told her that was what I wanted to get you Emma, a pure gold bead, and she found it! But she said it was the only one like it."

Nonno frowned. "That not real gold."

Penelope put her hands on her hips.

"Of course it's real."

Then Nonno took it from the palm of my hand, and before I could say anything, he popped it in his mouth and bit it.

"Okay. It real," he confirmed and spit it into a napkin.

"What did you go and do that for?" snapped Penelope. "I said it was real. Why would we get a fake gold bead all the way from Hong Kong?"

Nonno shooed her away as if she didn't know what she was talking about. Then he leaned over and slowly lifted Eggplant up into his lap. The dog remained asleep even when Nonno accidentally clunked her head against the table.

"Pay my attention. Gift from me and Eggplant Parmigiana."

"The dog?" whined Donatella. "Really, Nonno!"

"It's a cup of drool, I bet," said Penelope, who then giggled uncontrollably at her own joke.

Nonno ignored her comment and pulled Eggplant up to a sitting position. The only problem was the old dog was still sleeping and slipped back down into his lap.

"She tell you later," said Nonno. "Our gift, Emmaroni, is walk on beach *and* eat the popcorn box."

I couldn't help smiling.

"Thanks, Nonno."

"That's your present?" asked Penelope, scrunched up with disapproval. "That's what you always give her!"

But before Nonno could snap back at her, Donatella jumped up and cried, "Here comes the most fabulous present of the night!"

Not in all my twelve years could I remember my mother getting so excited over giving me something. Except maybe the time she bought me a costume tiara covered in glass diamonds, which she thought made me look like a real princess. But that was before I grew a foot in a year like a bamboo plant.

Donatella handed me the heavy box across the table past Penelope who was about to explode with anticipation. Wrapped in tons of sparkly tissue paper was an enormous hardcover volume entitled, *How to Learn at Home the Cosmic Way: Levels 6–12*, by Rhapsody Fig Merryweather.

I looked up at Donatella, a bit confused.

"How to learn *what* at home?"

Penelope had grabbed the box and was digging around looking to see if there was something else inside.

"Everything!" replied my mother as she swooped her arm in front of her exactly the way a fairy godmother grants a wish.

"Like what?" asked Penelope who dropped the empty box on the floor, just as baffled as I was.

My mother grabbed the book and turned to the table of contents.

"Read!"

I scanned the first page: Grade Level 6: Physical Science; Grade Level 6: Reading and Writing; Grade Level 6: Mathematics. . . . It went all the way up to Grade Level 12 subjects.

"But I already learn this stuff at school?"

"*That's* my present," exclaimed Donatella who was still standing. "No more awful, horrible, terrible school! Nonno is going to *homeschool* you at the library! Everyone's doing it!"

In total astonishment, I looked at my grandfather who was now asleep and snoring like his dog, both their heads hanging limply to one side.

"She doesn't have to go to school?!" screamed Penelope. "Man, that's what I'm gonna ask for. That's the best present *ever*!"

"Didn't I tell you?" replied my mother, who sank regally into her seat.

Penelope continued to shriek, "You're the luckiest kid in Homeport, Emma! My gold bead is already working!"

I stared at the strawberry cake, now fully thawed and melting into a mushy mess. Something definitely didn't feel right about this present. How did Donatella arrange all this? She had never attended one school assembly, even when I was the main monarch butterfly in the garden of wisdom in third grade. I'm not even sure she knew where my school was.

But at the same time, I also felt Penelope may be on to something. Maybe this was my lucky break. I didn't need school really. I honestly felt as if I already knew everything the teachers ever taught us. Why not teach myself?

On second thought, this *could* be the best gift I ever got.

F O U R

The day after my birthday was a Monday. I woke up at the usual time, 6:45, when I would get dressed for school. I always got ready by myself. Sometimes my grandfather and Eggplant were up just as I was leaving but never my mother. She normally slept until nine o'clock, an hour before the store opened at ten. Unless she had a late date.

But today was different. I stayed in bed and stared at the ceiling wondering what I was supposed to do next. Donatella said Nonno and I should discuss a schedule and figure out what I needed to learn. According to my mother, most home school kids did their bookwork at the library in the mornings and then interesting activities in the afternoons. Of course, she said, I already had an interesting afternoon activity. Working at the shop.

I decided to get up and make some breakfast. Normally I was in a rush and grabbed whatever I felt like eating, a cookie or a pudding. But today I thought I'd make a real breakfast like an omelet.

As I stood up, I caught a glimpse of myself in my bureau mirror. I couldn't believe how skinny and washed-out I was. And all the tiny freckles looked so weird, especially the ones on my face. Even worse, I noticed that the top of my head was cut off by the wooden frame. I moaned. When had that happened? I could always see my whole head in the mirror. Was I still growing? How big could I possibly get? At this rate, I was going to end up the tallest freak in the world.

I can't even remember the number of times people had asked me if I played basketball. I was so sick of that question. Maybe if I had, I would have fit in better at school. But I didn't even like basketball and never picked it to play in gym class. Just because I was tall, didn't mean I was any good. In fact, I generally stunk at sports. I doubt basketball would have been any different.

After I ate the eggs, I wondered if I should call the school to let them know I was never coming back. But then I remembered that Donatella said she had made all the arrangements, so they had to know. I would have loved to have seen Ms. Fiddle's face when they told her, "*Let's say this another way.* Emma quit school!"

The only thing on television was the news and little kids' shows. So I picked up *How to Learn at Home the Cosmic*

Way and flipped through the pages. I noticed the lesson plans were a bit different from the usual textbook examples. Instead of using names like Nate and Sarah in their word problems, these kids were Taurus and Meridian, astrological terms. No wonder Donatella liked this book.

I jumped ahead to the seventh-grade section and wasn't surprised to find it was super easy since it was the end of May and sixth grade was almost over. Plus I already knew I was pretty much brighter than the rest of my class. But then I read through the eighth-grade level and found that only a little less easy than the one before. Not until I looked through the eleventh grade chapters did I begin to feel challenged.

That's when it dawned on me. I could be finished with high school before I turned thirteen years old—

"Morning, Emma-roni!"

Nonno and Eggplant shuffled into the room. They both walked exactly the same way.

"Morning! Want an omelet?"

Suddenly I was in a great mood. Better than I had ever felt in my life! In an instant, the years and years of horrible, terrible school ahead of me had vanished. It almost seemed as if my life was just beginning.

Nonno clapped his hands together.

"Delizioso! Love the omelet!"

As I poured the yellow liquid into the piping hot pan, I slipped a glass of prune juice in front of my grandfather, who was reading the paper.

"So what time do you want to leave for the library?" I asked.

At first he didn't answer so I moved closer and said it again louder.

He looked down at Eggplant as if I were asking her.

"Library?"

"Remember, Nonno? You're taking me to the library every day to help homeschool me."

"Oh no, no library. All old women at library. All want to marry."

Then he cracked open his paper and continued to read as he ate the eggs.

It figured.

I knew Donatella hadn't really arranged anything at all. But at that point, I didn't care. It was still clear to me that I did not need school anymore. I just needed to make a precise list of things to do, which was the way I always organized my life when it was spinning out of control. Then I would go to the library by myself and finish the giant book on my own. Who knows, maybe I'd finish by the end of the month. And then I could apply to colleges if I wanted to or even get my own apartment.

After all, I was pretty sure I was done with being a kid. No wonder I felt and looked like a freak and had no friends other than Penelope, who was friends with everyone. Everything made sense now. At some point during the last year or so, I had skipped past everyone my age . . . and turned into an adult.

As far as I could tell, there were no home schooling students at the library. And the only old ladies were a couple of the librarians. In fact, I saw just two other people the whole time I was there.

I found a corner desk by the window that overlooked the port and part of Harbor Street. I leaned against the radiator and stared out at the view. The town of Homeport was quaint with brick walkways overgrown with vines and flowers. The antique buildings were various shapes and sizes, painted all sorts of crazy colors. The town was definitely cute, but it also seemed kind of messy to me. I mean, nothing matched. It was if the whole place were pieced together like an unplanned quilt made from leftover scraps.

In the distance beyond the port, filled with fishing boats and long piers, I could see the open ocean. It was kinda nice living by the water, particularly in the summer, but it also meant tons of crazy tourists. I couldn't stand it when they came into the shop, mixed up all the beads and then bought nothing.

When I opened *How to Learn at Home the Cosmic Way* and read the directions for Pre-Calculus Grade 11, I realized that Donatella had not bought the accompanying workbook. This volume only explained the concepts. The actual schoolwork was done in a second exercise book. I should have known.

I signed the sheet at the reference desk to use a computer and searched for the workbook on one of the bookseller websites. But the whole series was completely out of print. I turned to the front of my copy to look for the most recent publishing date—1979.

1979? Donatella was still a *real* high school cheerleader in 1979. Didn't she know a few things had changed since then?

I reminded myself that I was an adult now and needed to think like one. Adults talked to other adults all the time. I took a deep breath and pretended that I was working at the store to get up the courage to speak.

"Um. Excuse me?" I asked the librarian who was sitting in the middle of the large, round reference desk. She looked up from her graphic novel and smiled.

"Yes?"

"Could you recommend a home schooling textbook for grade 11?"

She politely studied me for a second as if she had no idea what I was talking about. Her hair was blond and frizzy to her waist, and she wore bright purple reading glasses along with an assortment of earrings up and down both ears.

"Is it for you?"

I nodded.

"Well, what have your parents selected?"

I showed her the *Cosmic Way*, and her eyes bugged out like it contained instructions on how to build a flying saucer.

"Oh my, where did they get this?"

I shrugged.

The librarian stood up. I was surprised to see she was as tall as I was, maybe even a bit taller. And she was wearing flats.

"Do you own a computer?"

I shook my head, no, embarrassed. "But I can come here every day and use one of yours."

She looked me up and down briefly, peering over the top of her glasses.

"You're in the eleventh grade, which means you're sixteen or seventeen?"

Her soft voice sounded a little suspicious. I stood up straighter.

"Sixteen," I lied.

"Okay" is all she said and then, "what's your name?"

I glanced down at my feet. "Emma."

She picked up the computer sign-up sheet and scanned the list.

"Emma Frrrra—Is that pronounced *Freak*?" she asked pointing to my signature.

Oh no, here it comes, I thought to myself as I slightly nodded.

"Is that your name? Am a Freak?"

I swear her eyes swept the library as if someone from a prank television show was about to leap out and confess it was all a joke. But then I told her what I always told people.

"My mother forgot to say it out loud when I was born."

The librarian grinned.

"Good answer," she said.

Then I didn't know what to say, so I said nothing.

"Well, Emma Freke—"

I cut her off, "Just Emma."

She smiled again. "Okay, Just Emma, come back tomorrow morning. I'll have some materials to get you started."

F I V E

The next morning, I got up a little later than usual since the library didn't open until 9:30. After breakfast and a shower, I decided to do some laundry. We had a small apartment-size washing machine but had to hang our clothes to dry on a retractable line that stretched from the front right corner to the bathroom.

"Thanks, you're a doll!"

Donatella was standing in the doorway of her bedroom in a long satin bathrobe, the color of pink bubble gum. Her black hair was piled on top of her head like cotton candy.

She stretched, then yawned loudly. "I've been meaning to wash those clothes all week."

"I don't mind doing it," I replied, which was mostly true since I knew all adults regularly did their own laundry . . . except my mother.

I grabbed a light jacket from the closet and my note-book from the coffee table.

"So see ya later."

"Hold on a millisecond!" said Donatella. "Where are you off to?"

My mother didn't know where I was 90 percent of *any* day, so I found it annoying when she occasionally stopped me to act like a parent.

"The library?" I answered with a question. "Remember, I'm homeschooling now?"

"Oh, that's right," she replied as she wandered over to the kitchen to pour a glass of wheatgrass juice. "How's that going? Is Nonno helpful?"

I almost told her exactly how it was going but decided to skip it. It wouldn't change anything.

"Fine and sort of."

To my surprise, Donatella set down her juice, strolled back across the room, and squeezed my cheeks with her stubby manicured fingers.

"Look at you, Emma!" she said as she pressed up on her tippy toes to pat the top of my head. "You're suddenly so . . . so . . . so . . . *grown up!*"

Regardless of the fact that I had been as tall as a street sign and doing everything on my own for more than a year, that was one of the most affectionate gestures my mother had made in a long time.

"Did you have a date last night or something?" I asked, wary of her wonderful mood.

She grinned. "How did you know?"

"Was it that Larry or Gary guy?"

"As a matter of fact," she said as she batted her eyelashes, which were still clumped with mascara from the night before, "I'm currently keeping company with Kevin."

"Kevin? The guy from the docks who was in the store last week?"

Donatella swept her bathrobe across her front and re-tied the satin belt tightly around her ample torso.

"Isn't he cute?" she giggled.

"Gross," I mumbled under my breath. For some reason, I really hoped this one wouldn't last long.

A gust of wind blew through the apartment. Donatella crossed the room, complaining.

"I keep telling Nonno to stop opening the windows at night! It's been so chilly lately."

The reference librarian was sitting at her round booth studying something in front of her. I didn't want to disturb her right away, so I settled down at the same corner desk I had chosen the day before. The library was very busy this morning with lots of little kids milling about with their parents. And way over on the other side of the building, a group of teenagers was gathered around a man who was holding a parrot. I wondered if they were on a field trip.

While I was waiting for the librarian to notice me, I decided to make one of my five-point lists. As I said before, making lists was kind of a hobby of mine, and they always included exactly five lines. For me, creating a list was as calming as sorting beads. I guess it was a way of organizing my meaningless life.

What You Need to Be an Adult

1. A home
2. Nice clothes
3. A job
4. A car
5. Tons of money

I stared at my neat handwriting and admired it. Each letter was consistently formed and spaced, every line uniform with the one above it. It was the one skill I was pretty proud of.

A blast of laughter echoed across the stacks and stacks of books. I turned around to see the older kids hovering around the large colorful bird. The parrot must have said something funny, I thought to myself. I leaned way back to get a better look.

"Good morning, Emma."

Just then the reference librarian slid a chair over from the next desk and sat with me. She wore a ruffly white blouse to her knees, and her long, frizzy hair was tied back in a loose ponytail. I counted only six earrings today.

"Oh, hi."

"I forgot to introduce myself yesterday. I'm Stevie."

She stuck out her hand for me to shake. I took it limply, not sure what to do. It dawned on me that "shaking hands" was something I should have included on my list of adult stuff.

"Stevie?" I was confused. "Isn't that a boy's—" I stopped myself.

"A boy's name?" she asked, finishing my question. Then she smiled. "You know names and words hurt only if you let them."

I wasn't quite sure what she meant by that, but then Stevie changed the subject.

"Before we get started this morning, there are a few things I need to clarify."

I assumed she wanted to give me an assessment test to find out exactly how advanced I was. Or maybe I had to fill out forms with my address and my mother's name.

"Sure," I replied.

"I called the school yesterday, Emma. They knew nothing about your homeschooling and said you've been absent since last Friday."

The library began to spin a little. I stared down at my hands. They were trembling, which always happened when I knew someone was upset with me.

"They also said that you're only in the sixth grade."

S I X

"Are they gonna arrest you?"

Penelope and I were nervously perched on my single bed with the door closed. The head guidance counselor from the school district, a member from the school committee, my mother, and Nonno were all having a meeting at the kitchen table. We couldn't hear anything other than serious-sounding murmurs.

"If they arrest anyone," I whispered, "it should be Donatella for giving her only kid a fake birthday present."

Penelope just shook her head. What could she say? No one else we knew had a lunatic for a mother.

Earlier that day at the library, after Stevie had informed me that she had called the school to make sure I wasn't "truant" (which means "skipping"), I burst out crying. Something I hadn't done in public since my hamster,

Pippy, had died when I was eight. But I couldn't help myself. I knew deep down Donatella had never officially removed me from the school, so I wasn't really surprised. But the thought of going back sounded worse than going to prison.

Stevie had led me to the private library staff lounge where she made two cups of peppermint tea. After I caught my breath, she asked why I pretended to be older than twelve.

That's when it all came pouring out.

I don't know why I chose to confess all the miserable details of my pathetic life to someone I had just met. I guess no one, other than Penelope, had ever shown a real interest in me or my feelings. Ms. Fiddle didn't count. She was always *telling* me how I should feel instead of asking.

Then, to my surprise, Stevie said that she knew exactly what I was going through. That she too was the tallest kid in her grade (and the grade above). When I told her that it was more than being mega-vertical—that I had nothing in common with kids my age—she just smiled and nodded. It was like she really knew how I felt.

But now, trembling in my bedroom hours later, it seemed Stevie was the one who had completely destroyed my life by calling the school. As Penelope and I huddled together on my beige bedspread, I wondered if it was possible to run away or, at the very least, hide in Penelope's house until everything blew over. Perhaps the Gray Moms would take pity on me.

The door to my bedroom cracked open, and Donatella peered in. Penelope stood up on the bed.

"Is Emma going to the slammer?"

My mother smirked.

"Don't be ridiculous. But it's time for you to run home, little girl."

I felt nauseous. Oh no. Were they sending me back to school?

"*Please* let me stay," Penelope begged with praying hands. "I won't say a word, I promise."

"Emma will phone you later. Now scoot!"

Penelope hugged my waist good-bye like she might never see me again. I even noticed her eyes were wet with tears. As she left the apartment, I could hear her loud sniffles all the way down the stairs.

I dragged myself over to the table of somber adults who stared at me. At that moment, I didn't feel grown up at all. I glanced at Nonno, who was studying his lap as if hiding a book under his napkin. I had a feeling he thought he had done something wrong but had no idea what it was. When I sat down, Eggplant waddled over and licked my sneakers.

"Who would like some boiled ginseng root?" asked Donatella. The kettle was already whistling on the stove.

Everyone mumbled, no thank you.

"Emma," began the man across from me, grinning hard through crowded, yellow teeth, "my name is Mr. Millfoil—*Mill* like a wind*mill* and *foil* like aluminum *foil*—and I am in charge of the guidance department for K through 12 in Homeport!"

I couldn't help staring at him. The front part of his scalp was bald and shiny, but brown tufts of hair stuck out in back, and he had a mustache that turned up like fish hooks at both ends. He looked as if he might have been a circus clown in another life.

"And I'm Miss McFight with the Homeport school committee," said the woman next to him. She had tiny eyes and wore the teensiest earrings I had ever seen.

All at once, a disgusting pair of odors met above the table. It was the combination of ginseng steaming in Donatella's cup and Eggplant's urgent need to go for a walk. The two guests tried to cover their noses without anyone noticing.

Nonno jumped up, obviously relieved to get out of the apartment.

"Nature call! Be back *pronto*."

He slipped on the dog's leash and hobbled down the stairs on his cane as fast as he could.

"We need to wrap it up soon, if you don't mind," said Donatella, checking her chunky square watch. "I have a client in fifteen minutes."

"Oh, are you a therapist, Mrs. Freke?" asked the school committee lady.

"Bead-ologist, amongst many other intuitive talents," replied Donatella.

The two guests stared blankly for a second.

"Okay then!" began Mr. Millfoil, as he clapped his hands loudly. "It recently came to our attention, Emma, that you were under the impression, or *mis*impression, that we had granted you, Emma, permission to be home-schooled by your grandfather, Mr. Salvoni."

He spoke slowly in a very careful, choppy way.

"As I told you before, it was my birthday present to her," said Donatella, stirring her cup of smelly potion and grinning contentedly.

"Telling a child they no longer have to go to school should not be positioned as a *gift*," said Miss McFight.

"It was the *perfect* gift for Emma," my mother barked. "She absolutely despises school."

Our guests looked at one another and rolled their eyes.

At that point, I realized things were about as bad as they could possibly get. Even I knew that everything my mother said was the opposite of what a normal parent should say. Thankfully, she didn't take this stressful moment to offer anyone a foot massage.

"Regardless of your approach, Mrs. Freke," said the guidance counselor, "there are specific steps you must take in order to receive permission to homeschool your child."

"That's absurd," said Donatella as she waved her hand at them. "In case you didn't know, this is a free country."

"With laws that protect children," said the school committee member.

"If Emma needs any protection, she needs it at that miserable school! Do you know that she doesn't have one single friend there?"

How did she know that? I wondered. But then I started to cough as loudly as I could. Anything to get Donatella to stop talking. She turned and banged me on the back as if I were choking.

"Which leads us to our *pro*-posal," said Mr. Millfoil, who smiled broadly at Miss McFight as if reminding her to remain calm.

"That's right, *Emma*," she said sharply. "We have decided that since there are fewer than two weeks until the end of the school year, it would be acceptable for you to take a mini leave of absence. You may finish up your sixth-grade lessons under the professional guidance of a school-appointed tutor."

So they weren't going to send me back? I could hardly believe my ears. Donatella nodded confidently as if she had somehow won this battle.

"However," said Mr. Millfoil, "for reasons we have carefully calculated and seriously surmised, we will not recommend a home school program for you in the coming year. Instead, Ms. Fiddle, the school psychologist—as you know an award-winning and outstanding expert in her field—would like to administer your registration at an appropriate academic environment for you to resume your studies in the fall."

"What does that mean exactly?" asked Donatella, warily eyeing them both.

"It means," said Mr. Millfoil, grinning so hard I could see his puffy gums, "that Emma has been referred to our new partner program for, what we like to call, *special students.*"

Then he added, "I think they might even have a basketball team!"

S E V E N

"Oh man, Emma!" cried Penelope. "They're sending you to the nuthouse for kids!"

We were licking ice cream cones later that afternoon down on the central pier. Mine was vanilla. Penelope had a double scoop of raspberry bear claw with sprinkles.

I had never heard of a nuthouse for kids and assumed she was making it up.

"What are you talking about?"

"It's about an hour from here. Cynthia used to work there part-time before I started pinching people at preschool for attention. Then she and Katherine decided a parent should be home with me all day."

I crunched on my cone as I studied a seagull a few feet away. He was waiting patiently for leftovers.

"Why would they send me there? I'm not nuts. If anything, I'm totally boring."

"Think about it," said Penelope, her full dark lips smeared with creamy red ice cream. "You go to Ms. Fiddle twice a week, *and* they've met Donatella, the nuttiest mother on the planet!"

All of a sudden, I lost my appetite. I stood up and threw the rest of the cone in the trash because I knew better than to feed the gulls. (They were supposed to eat fish and natural stuff, not people food.) I peered over the edge and saw my reflection in the water. I looked like a scary giant, like some sea monster lurking in the waves. Maybe I was insane.

I quickly turned away from myself.

"Do you really think that's what they meant?"

Penelope finished her entire cone before answering.

"Well, just to be on the safe side, this is what you should do."

She stood up and paced importantly up and down the pier, rubbing her sticky palms together. The seagull followed her assuming he was about to finally get his treat.

"Tomorrow, when you meet your tutor, smile a lot and talk about all your friends."

"But I'm only friends with you," I corrected her anxiously.

Penelope stopped with her hands on her hips.

"You got to work with me, Emma!"

"Okay I got it, lots of friends."

"And chat up going to the movies and the mall and junk."

Penelope continued to pace.

"Why?"

"So you sound normal!"

I frowned.

"But where will this all get me?" I asked. "Back at middle school?"

Penelope licked her lips, then wiped her mouth with a napkin from her pocket. Out of nowhere, a gust of salty ocean air twirled up the pier and blew the seagull away.

"I haven't thought it all the way through yet," she said like a detective on a difficult case. "But don't worry. The Gray Moms always say everything works out in the end."

The Gray Moms did seem to know a lot, at least according to Penelope. But this time, I wasn't so sure.

That night I made a five-point list, just to be on the safe side.

How to Sound Normal

1. Mention lots of fake friends
2. Pretend to love the mall
3. Talk about all the movies I'm dying (not) to see
4. Try to giggle
5. Apply lip gloss frequently

I was told to meet my school-appointed tutor at the library at noon everyday for three hours until I finished the sixth-grade curriculum. Which was fine with except that I didn't want to run into Stevie. I was pretty steamed at her. After all, if she hadn't called the school, no one would have noticed that I quit. And Mr. Millfoil and Miss McFight wouldn't have shown up at our apartment interfering in my life.

I realized I had no way of knowing who my tutor was, so I sat down at an open table to watch for a tutorlike person to walk through the doors. Then it occurred to me that I would be easy to spot. Just look for the freak with bright red hair.

"Emma?"

Ugh. It was Stevie. I slumped over and leaned on my arm turning away from her.

"Hi," I mumbled.

She was probably wondering why I wasn't back at school.

"It's good to see you!"

I still refused to look at her and opened my notebook as if I had something to do.

"Yep."

There was silence for about ten long seconds. Then I heard that blast of laughter from the day before. Without thinking, I twisted around and saw the same group of teenagers across the building. They were standing around a sculpture by a fountain. I wondered who they were and what was so funny.

When I turned back, I noticed Stevie was watching me.

"Should we get started?" she asked.

Now I looked directly at her.

"On your schoolwork?" she said. "The guidance counselor dropped off everything you need to do to finish the year."

"You're my tutor?"

It turns out Stevie had called back the school after our cup of tea in the staff room. She was the one who had suggested my "mini leave of absence" for the remainder of the year. And since she was the reference librarian, they didn't hesitate to take her up on her offer to tutor me. Besides, Ms. Fiddle was out with the chicken pox so they had no idea who was going to "oversee my file."

That first afternoon, we actually got through four days' worth of geography and social studies in three hours. We even talked a little about it. I often had questions about science and history and stuff but never had anyone to ask. The discussions at school were so pitiful. No one even seemed to know the difference between the Revolutionary War and the Industrial Revolution.

"You were right, Emma," said Stevie as I stood to leave at three o'clock. "You are advanced. Quite advanced for your age. You asked terrific questions."

"Thanks."

All at once, I panicked. I had forgotten everything on my list. I didn't mention any friends or the mall or the movies. And I never once giggled or used the lip gloss I borrowed from Donatella's makeup chest. The only thing

Stevie knew about me was that I hated school. And that I was pretty smart.

"Stevie?"

She looked up from my pile of completed work and grinned.

"More questions?"

"Just one. Is there a school near here that's really a nuthouse for kids?"

She pursed her lips and pondered as if she wasn't sure how to answer.

"I guess there's probably a school for everyone."

Someone rang the bell at the reference desk so Stevie jumped up and rushed away.

"See you tomorrow, Emma—same time!"

E I G H T

That afternoon the shop was busier than usual. First, a mom wanted to buy beads for a bunch of girls to make necklaces at her daughter's birthday party. Since they were inviting fifteen kids, they needed a ton and lots of variety. And the mom didn't seem to care about the cost. Then there were two old ladies who had recently taken a work-shop from Donatella. They had an Aztec pattern that included matching bracelets. A few other regular customers had odds and ends to pick up. Then my mother's fishing "friend," Kevin, rushed in just as I was about to close the store. He pushed the door shut against the strong wind, which was picking up again outside.

"Hey there," he grunted. "I was in the other day?"

There was something I didn't like about this guy, but I couldn't figure out what it was exactly.

"Um. Donatella isn't around. I'm not sure when she'll be back."

Not a minute later, that tall, bald businessman from the week before slipped in too, wearing the exact same black suit. I groaned to myself, convinced he had bad news. Now I'd never get to close up.

"Well, me and 'Tella are meeting up tonight at Seaweed Sam's for supper," said Kevin. "Let her know I'll be late, got it?"

Seaweed Sam's was a run-down bar with no windows. I didn't know they actually served food.

"Sure, if I see her," I replied.

I decided not to count the money in front of two virtual strangers. Instead, I closed all the blinds and reversed the OPEN sign.

"Oh yeah, I forgot," said Kevin. "You're probably punching out the old time card and going home to wherever you live, huh?"

I glanced over at the man in the suit who I could tell was pretending to be interested in the beads. But I was sure he was about to inform me that our taxes were overdue or my mother had lost her retail license. I slid covers over the bead compartments, making it obvious that it was time for everyone to leave.

"Well I'm not going far," I replied to Kevin as I watched the other guy. "Home for me is up the stairs."

The man in the suit paused and twisted his head toward us.

"Wait!" said Kevin. "You live here too?" he asked, sounding confused. "Are you 'Tella's roommate?"

Roommate? I stopped what I was doing. I couldn't believe my ears.

"She's my *mother*?"

Kevin's jaw dropped just a little. Then he scratched his head and started to laugh nervously.

"Oh, I get it," he whispered in a raspy voice. "On second thought, no message. But ah, thanks for the information."

And as Kevin turned to leave, I noticed the man in the dark suit was already gone.

Later that night, I woke up and heard crying out in the Big Room. The television volume was way too loud. I crept out of bed and cracked the door open. Nonno was sound asleep in his old brown plaid recliner with Eggplant snoring on his lap. The couch faced the TV, and I could just see the back of Donatella's head over the puffy cushion. Everything shook as she blew her nose extra hard. She was watching some old movie.

I tiptoed over and sat in the rocking chair close to the sofa. Donatella tried smiling at me, but she couldn't hide that she had been sobbing. Long black streaks of mascara tears flowed down her cheeks as all her makeup merged together and formed little rivers.

"The movie," she said as she blew again into a hankie. "It's a sad one."

I glanced at the television. The show didn't seem sad. It was one of those old-fashioned martial arts films starring that guy who now pretends to be a politician.

Donatella and I never talked about our emotions. We just steered clear of each other when we weren't feeling so great. Usually, when she was in one of these moods, she locked herself in her bedroom and didn't come out until she was fully recovered. Occasionally, when she was having a really bad bout, it could last as long as three days.

"The store was busy this afternoon," I said to cheer her up.

"Was it?" she replied, sighing loudly.

"I think we made over three hundred dollars."

She sniffed and blew.

"Did you put it in the safe?"

"Yep," I replied.

Just then gunfire erupted on the television set. It woke up Nonno who thought someone was shooting at us.

"*Mia spada!*" he yelled, practically pushing Eggplant off his lap.

"Simmer down!" Donatella hollered back. "You don't need your sword, Nonno. It's a movie! Just go to bed, will ya!"

Mumbling in Italian, my grandfather rubbed his face and then rubbed the dog's face before lowering her to the ground. He carefully folded in his recliner, picked up his cane, and hoisted himself up like he weighed a thousand pounds. Finally, the two of them shuffled off to the loft. The whole procedure took about five minutes.

My mother stood and gathered up her things.

"I guess we should get some shut-eye too, Emma."

That's when I remembered to tell her about Kevin's visit.

"Oh by the way, your friend stopped in the shop today just as I was closing."

Donatella twisted around. "Which friend?"

"That Kevin person."

"He did? Why didn't you tell me?"

"Because he said you were meeting for dinner and that he didn't need to leave a message."

She crossed her arms.

"Then why did he stop in if he didn't need to leave a message? Was he buying beads?"

All at once, Donatella sounded super annoyed. That's when I realized I shouldn't have brought it up.

"Well, at first he was going to leave a message that he would be late for dinner. But then he decided not to leave that message and left."

"But that doesn't make any sense," she snapped, "*plus* he stood me up!"

"Well, don't get mad at me—he's creepy anyway!"

My hands began to tremble. This is why I never had these kinds of conversations with my mother. In the end, I always felt like everything was somehow my fault.

"*Emma*. You MUST have said something to change his mind."

She stomped over to the TV and turned it off.

"All I said was that I lived upstairs and I wasn't sure if I'd see you before dinner."

"You mean you told him you were *my daughter*?"

"Not exactly—but I'm sure he figured it out."

"No wonder!" she cried over and over again, banging her forehead with her fist.

"No wonder what?"

But she didn't answer me. Instead, my forty-seven-year-old mother burst into tears like a blubbering baby. She ran across the floor and slammed her bedroom door behind her.

And she didn't come out—at least when I was around—for three full days.

Which Subjects are Off-Limits with Donatella

1. Her dates
2. Her past
3. Her weight
4. Her daughter
5. Her life

N I N E

Between working the store in the morning, tutoring in the mid afternoon, then working the store again until it closed at 6:00 P.M.—not to mention doing all the cooking and cleaning—I was busier than most grown-ups. As soon as it became obvious that my mother wasn't coming out of her room for those three days, I decided it was up to me to keep things together until she got better. Especially since everything was obviously my fault. Nonno didn't even seem to notice Donatella was missing as long as he got dinner at night. As for the shop, I taped a sign to the door when I left for the library: "Back at 3 P.M."

"Think about it from *his* point of view—," said Penelope. A new shipment of African beads had arrived, which I had saved for her to open. She took a penknife out of her pocket and carefully sliced the edges of the box as she spoke.

"—this guy, Kevin, thinks he's dating a woman without any baggage. Next thing he knows, not only does she have a kid, but he's guessing this kid is like twenty years old, which would make Donatella something like sixty or seventy. And I bet all along she's been telling him she's only thirty!"

I was sweeping the floor and hunting for any beads that may have popped out of their cubbies.

"But her other dates always knew that I was her daughter."

"And did *they* last?" asked Penelope in a squeaky kid voice (contrasting with her grown-up advice). "Donatella is realizing she has *got* to change her strategy if she wants a man. She's no spring chicken anymore. And no offense, Emma, but you're not helping her image at all."

I swept the dust out the front door, but most of it was blown back in by the wind.

"Do you really think that's what this is all about?"

Penelope pried open the carton carefully and lifted out the small interior boxes.

"Believe me, it happens all the time."

I could never figure out how Penelope knew so much about life. She seemed to soak up street smarts like a dry sponge.

"How do you know it happens all the time?" I asked.

"When Cynthia is napping in the afternoon, I sometimes turn on those talk shows. Man, there are a lot of people out there lying and misrepresenting themselves."

I knew that even if that was true, I couldn't help it that I was Donatella's unlucky kid and that I appeared a whole generation older than I actually was. Why did I get punished for everything?

Then Penelope said quietly, "Emma? I've been meaning to ask you something—"

But then she stopped herself and whistled long and sweetly.

"Look at these *beeeeeauuuties*!"

Inside the first small white box were polished clay beads painted in glossy, vibrant colors. And every one of these beautiful beads was decorated with a different miniature bird. Even the holes, which tunneled through the beads, were outlined in wonderful shades of red.

"Can you imagine being able to make something so pretty?" she wondered aloud.

We sat down and looked through all the small cartons. Each design was as equally amazing as the one before it.

When we were done sorting, Penelope stuck her whole head in the shipping box.

"And it all smells so *good*!" she cried from inside the box.

I had to giggle.

"What's it smell like?"

She lifted her head, grinning blissfully.

"Africa."

The third and final day of Donatella's self-exile was a Friday. I was sitting at the big table at the library finishing an English essay—"Symbolism of the Wheel in *Tuck Everlasting* by Natalie Babbitt"—wondering if I should tell Stevie about my strange week. She was over in the stacks helping a woman find choices for her book club to read.

The group of teenagers was nowhere in sight today. They seemed to come a few times a week, but the days varied. By now I knew they weren't on a field trip since they visited the library so often, but they were always accompanied by the same teacher. I had studied them enough to know there were five boys and three girls in the group. I guessed they were around thirteen to sixteen years old. But who was I to guess someone's age?

I had been thinking a lot lately about that nuthouse for kids where Penelope's Gray Mom, Cynthia, used to work. In fact, I had searched it on a library computer, and the only thing I came up with was a school over in the next county for children (five to twelve) with "moderate to severe neurological and spectrum disorders." First of all, I didn't have either of those things as far as I knew. Plus I was now twelve, almost too old for the age range. And finally, it said nothing about kids who were disturbed or nutty.

Still, there was a link on the website to a facility for "semi-functioning adults." Was that what I was? A semi-adult?

For a few days, I had been convinced that I had skipped over childhood straight into the world of grown-ups. But now I was doubting my own theory. It was true that adults were easier for me to talk to. They weren't rude and mean like most kids. But even though I didn't get along with people my age, I realized I had even less in common with grown-ups. They were just so clueless. Except Stevie. But I had a feeling she was one of those people, like Penelope, who everyone felt comfortable around. No matter what their ages.

I was no longer mad at Stevie. After all, she had only been doing her job when she called the school to check on me. For all she knew, I could have been a runaway or a juvenile delinquent. Truthfully, in the last few days, I had grown to like her a lot. She had so many cool interests, like kayaking and antiquing and weaving. In fact, when I told her about our shop, she said she would stop in to buy some beads for her textiles.

On some level, I felt like Stevie and I were related. She seemed to truly understand me. We even sat the same way with our legs crossed tightly so that one ankle wrapped around the other. And then there was our mutual height as well as the whole awkward name thing we both shared.

It had occurred to me more than once that I might end up alone like Stevie. I mean, I assumed she was alone since she never mentioned anybody else. And maybe living alone would be kind of nice. I definitely knew how to take care of myself. I could cook, clean, and do the laundry. I also had things that interested me like lots of academic subjects and, of course, the beads. And come to think of it, I could pretty much run a business all by myself.

"Are you done, Emma?" Stevie was back. She sat down and glanced over my paper. "May I read it?"

"Sure," I said. "It's finished."

She smiled and patted my arm.

"Do you know what this means?" she asked.

"That we're done for the day?"

"Better than that!" she exclaimed. "We're done for the *year*! Unless you just bombed this paper, which I doubt, you are forever done with the sixth grade."

"I am? But don't I have one more week? I thought school got out next Friday?"

"It does, but you have nothing left to do. You sailed through your courses. Congrats!"

She put her hand out to shake mine, and this time, I squeezed and shook as hard as I could.

I gathered my things and stood to leave.

"So I guess I won't be seeing you for a while?"

Stevie looked up from my paper.

"Whyever not?" She pushed her chair back and crossed her legs in that familiar way. "Don't you like coming to the library?"

"Well, yah," I answered.

"Then take the weekend off, and I'll see you Monday at noon. We have to have our end-of-the-year party!"

I had an idea.

"Could we meet at three o'clock instead?"

"Sure," she said, "if that's easier. However, it does get busier in the afternoon."

"I just thought it might be fun to bring a friend," I explained.

Stevie grinned. "Even better!"

TEN

I waited by the display window at the shop for Penelope to arrive. It was fifteen minutes before three o'clock, and I didn't want to be late for my end-of-the-year party.

It's funny. At middle school, I dreaded any event like the last day of school or the afternoon before spring break or any unstructured time where students were allowed to mingle and ... gab. But all weekend, I had grown more and more excited about Monday afternoon, mostly because I couldn't wait for Penelope and Stevie to meet.

Thankfully, everything was back to normal (if you can call it that) in our apartment. Late Friday night, exactly three days after locking herself in her bedroom, Donatella flung open her door, dressed for a night on the town.

"Don't wait up, kiddos!" she cried so loudly that she momentarily woke Nonno and Eggplant. They were sitting together, as usual, in their brown plaid recliner.

I sat near them on the sofa sewing a button back onto my shirt. I really needed some new clothes—everything was getting too tight and, of course, too short.

At first I was hesitant to meet Donatella's eyes so I continued with my sewing. But she marched directly over to me and punched my arm as if nothing had ever happened between us.

"What are you making?" she asked. She was chomping loudly on a wad of gum, something she often did when she was wound up.

I took a deep breath and peered up at her.

"Nothing. I'm just sewing a button back on a shirt."

"Aren't you clever!" she hollered too loudly.

Her ink black hair was loose and poufy with an imitation diamond barrette pinned to the side of her head. I had never seen the dress before, a polka-dot pattern that wrapped around her waist in a complicated way. Make-up covered every inch of her face and an enormous pear-shaped green crystal pendant dangled on the end of a necklace.

It occurred to me that Donatella never wore any of the beads we sold. For that matter, neither did I. I sometimes made a bracelet or earrings to sell in our showcase, but I never thought to actually wear them.

"So where are you off to?" I asked. I really didn't care. I was just relieved to see her back to her old self.

She slipped a ruby red cape over her shoulders and buckled the large clasp around her neck.

"Got a date!" she announced between blowing a bubble and popping it with her teeth.

"Kevin?"

Did I just say that? How could I have let his name slip out of my mouth! And at the top of my list on *which subjects are off-limits* were Donatella's dates!

But luckily, she seemed completely recovered.

"Nah, Kevin has some hang-up about kids," she said as she shook something out of one of her high heels. "Too complicated for him," she whined, making little quotation marks in the air.

So Penelope was right. No wonder I didn't like the guy.

"Sorry," I said.

"His loss," she winked then popped her gum. "But tonight I'm seeing Antonio!"

The Italian roll of the tongue woke Nonno again.

"That's a *good* boy!" he said pointing at the ceiling. Then he drifted back into a slumber.

Donatella cocked her head, winked at me, and said, "I guess we'll just have to wait and see."

Ugh. Gross. I sort of hoped he didn't like kids either.

I watched Penelope run diagonally across the street, where Driftwood and Harbor intersected. She wore a fancy blue dress trimmed with lace and bows that made her look even younger than she already was. She seemed to be having difficulty pushing through the wind while balancing a large tray covered in plastic wrap.

"What's that?" I asked as I opened the shop door.

"Coconut fudge truffles," she grimaced as if they were chocolate covered nails. "Cynthia insisted on making them for your party. There's enough for everyone in the whole library *and* the town hall put together!"

"You didn't have to get dressed up," I commented. "Do you want to change?"

"If I go back there, I'm telling you, those Gray Moms will make me wear a crown."

I let myself chuckle a little. After all, it was pretty funny. Here I was grateful that my mother left her bedroom to join the real world again, while Penelope had more motherly attention and fussing than she could stand.

When we arrived at the library, Stevie was at her circular desk with an elderly couple who were researching their genealogy, so she asked us to wait for a bit. I noticed she glanced twice at Penelope in her puffy party dress lugging the huge silver tray.

Stevie put her arms out.

"Would you like me to keep that here for you?"

"Please!" said Penelope as she dropped the truffles with a thud on the reference desk. The elderly couple smiled.

"You can have one," Penelope offered. She pulled back the plastic wrap. "You can have all of them!"

The old people each took a candy and smiled a silent thank you.

"We really aren't supposed to eat in the library," Stevie whispered to me. "Why don't you take these back into the lounge, Emma?"

I felt very important leading Penelope behind the circulation desk to the Staff Only area. And she was impressed with the employee room, which included a full kitchen, a leather couch, and four matching leather armchairs.

"You're really allowed to come back here? Man, I like this place."

I set the tray in the middle of the coffee table and wrote "Take One" on a piece of paper.

Back in the library, we waited for Stevie at the large glass table where I usually did my schoolwork. Just then that same group of eight teens and their teacher started clapping on the other side of the building.

"Are you allowed to make that much noise in the library?" asked Penelope, straining around in her seat to stare at them.

Her blue dress stuck straight out over her legs, and I could see that her feet didn't reach the floor. I realized I had not been Penelope's size in a very long time. It seemed as if it felt so safe to be so small. I, on the other hand, was like a gigantic target visible from outer space.

"For some reason, *they're* allowed to do whatever they want," I said. "They're here a lot and do all sorts of things."

"Who are they?" she wanted to know.

I shrugged and glanced back at Stevie. It looked as if she may be stuck for a while.

"Well what are they doing today?" asked Penelope, kicking the air with her shiny dress-up shoes.

"Beats me," I mumbled. I was wondering if I should ask Stevie if she wanted us to come back later.

Next thing I knew, Penelope slid off her chair and marched directly toward the group of teens who were now oohing and aahing at something or someone.

"Penelope! *Penelope!*" I whispered as loudly as I could. But she didn't hear me and continued to stride confidently in her blue party dress toward the action on the other side of the library.

I was so embarrassed, I couldn't bear to watch. Why was she always doing stuff like this?

"Where's your friend?" asked Stevie.

I sighed.

"Um. Bathroom."

"Well, I freed up my schedule so we could go out to celebrate—somewhere like the new Café Anchor. Have you been there? They have delicious scones."

"No, but sounds good."

We waited for a few awkward minutes. I figured Penelope had the sense to come back as soon as she figured out what the older kids were up to. But then a splash of laughter washed across the building. And in all that commotion, I could tell which laugh belonged to her.

Stevie stretched her neck to peer over at the group of happy kids.

"Hey, isn't that your friend?"

Slowly, I turned around. There she was being held up in the air, flat on her back, by the eight teenagers. Her blue dress glowing like a neon sign.

"Let's join her over in the Observatory and see what they're up to!" said Stevie in a voice that was a little too chipper.

This was *exactly* the kind of situation I dreaded more than anything in the entire world. And Penelope knew it. I was so upset with her right now that I wasn't sure I would ever speak to her again. This was my party, my day, and now it was ruined.

I followed Stevie across the carpeted floor to a separate domed area called the Observatory. Since we were the same height, I felt like I could slump behind her. I was completely aware of my too tight shirt and too short jeans and too pale skin and the very red bun in the back of my head. I crossed my arms and tried not to scowl.

"Gordon!"

"Hi Stevie!"

Gordon, the teacher, was handing out paper to all the kids including Penelope. They were now rushing around a table filled with tools and supplies, grabbing this and that.

"Okay everybody," said Gordon. "I want you all to measure the strength of your hands using the drop weights. Then record your findings. Except you," he said pointing at Penelope. "We need to weigh you on the scale."

"Awesome!" Penelope cried.

I couldn't believe this was happening.

Gordon walked over to us, and Stevie introduced me using my whole horrifying name. For some reason, I couldn't lift my head. My gaze was glued to the ground. It took all my willpower not to throw up.

"Want to join us, Emma?" he asked. "We're trying to prove, using physics, how stage diving works when people are moshing at a rock concert."

I had barely heard of "stage diving" or "moshing," whereas not-even-ten-year-old Penelope appeared to be a professional. The sad truth was, I happened to be in-telligent about some things, but for some reason, I never retained basic tweenage cultural knowledge. And that's exactly why I dreaded being forced into these social situa-tions. Ms. Fiddle could counsel me until her eyes popped out of her head. . . . I would never fit in at school.

Luckily, Stevie came to my rescue.

"Actually, Gordon, we're heading out for a little cel-ebration of our own. We just came over to fetch our friend in the pretty dress."

"Listen up, people!" said Gordon as he snapped his fingers.

All of a sudden, I felt as if I might faint *and* throw up.

"You all know Stevie, we just met Penelope, and so this is Emma *Freke*. Can everyone say 'Hi' to *Am a Freak*!"

I couldn't believe this was happening. It was like some middle school nightmare. The library began to spin as I braced myself.

"Hey! Hi there! Hello, Emma!"

I peeked over Stevie's shoulder.

Every single teenager was smiling at me.

"I know Emma!" yelled Penelope. "She's the smartest, nicest kid in the whole world, *and* she's my best friend!"

ELEVEN

"Man, this is delicious!"

Penelope was leaning over her plate of Boston Crème pie at Café Anchor and devouring it as if she hadn't eaten in days. Her blue hair ribbons were coming loose and slipping down her braids.

"I come to this place every chance I get," said Stevie.

She was eating a cranberry lemon scone with coddled cream and a cup of espresso.

I had chosen an oatmeal cookie.

"From now on, *I'm* coming here every chance I get!" said Penelope.

I was still trying to sort out what had happened back at the library. I wasn't that upset with anyone anymore, but the whole scene had left a queasy, shameful feeling in my stomach. And my heart was still racing. It was so strange how nice those kids were to me, especially after hearing my whole weird name *twice*. Did they really mean it, or were they forced to act like that? And I couldn't stay mad at Penelope for putting me in that situation. She couldn't help being super sociable any more than I could control my freakiness . . . and in the end, she stuck up for me in front of everyone.

"So what are your plans for the summer, Penelope?" asked Stevie. "Will you be going to camp?"

"Let me tell you, my Gray Moms have everything mapped out," she said sticking up her fingers to count off her activities.

"I got horseback riding lessons, I got swimming lessons, I got tennis lessons, I got African dance camp for two weeks, I got musical theater camp for two more weeks, and then we're taking our annual surprise trip. They never tell me where we're going until we get to the airport. They like to see *the thrill* written all over my face."

I forgot that Penelope was either gone or overscheduled during the summer. Every year, just when I thought I would be happy to be out of school, my one and only friend disappeared for most of the vacation.

Stevie grinned warmly at Penelope and laughed in between her finger counting. I was glad that the two of them had finally met, but I also felt kind of jealous. What was it that people loved so much about Penelope? And why didn't I have any of whatever it was that made her so . . . appealing?

"What's your favorite thing to do out of all those activities?" asked Stevie.

"None of the above," answered Penelope as she scooped up the last bite of pie and took a long slurp of strawberry milk. "My most favorite thing is to go to the beach and bodysurf the waves! But sometimes we're so busy in the summer, I don't even get the chance to do that. And the ocean is right down the street!"

"Well, I bet a lot of kids wouldn't mind being in your shoes," said Stevie.

You can say that again, I thought to myself. I was nibbling on my cookie. It was dry. I wished I had thought to get a glass of water.

"So what are *you* doing this summer, Stevie?" asked Penelope. She had a serious adult expression on her face, like a professor or a scientist, and rubbed her chin.

Stevie giggled.

"Well, thank you for asking, Penelope. I'll spend most of my days at the library. But in the summers, we close on Fridays, so I get a bunch of three-day weekends. That's when I go up to northern Maine to meet friends of mine, and we camp under the stars and kayak on all the beautiful ocean inlets. And I'll also fly home to Oregon at some point to see my family."

"I didn't know all that," I said.

Stevie tilted her head. "Didn't know all what, Emma?"

"That you liked to camp and that you had friends in Maine and that your family was in Oregon. I didn't even know you had a family."

"Doesn't everybody have a family *somewhere* in the world?" asked Penelope.

Stevie smiled. "You would think so."

I thought about what it would be like to have no family at all. And for some reason, it didn't sound so bad to me. After all, my family barely knew I existed.

Then Stevie asked, "What about you, Emma?"

"Huh?"

"Are you doing anything special over vacation?"

I glanced at Penelope who stared down at her empty plate. She knew that nothing special ever happened to me.

"Um. I'll just be working in the bead shop, I guess."

We stopped at the library to get Cynthia's silver tray. Most of the coconut fudge truffles had been eaten by the staff, so we placed the remainder on a paper plate.

Penelope held the shiny tray in front of us, which made a fuzzy mirror image of our two faces. Beyond our sizes, I never realized how super different we looked . . . and how pretty Penelope was, especially standing next to me. But instead of pointing out my dreadfully droopy features or bizarre freckles, Penelope swung her arm around my waist and blurted into the tray, "Look at that, BFFs!"

It was almost as if she saw something else.

We said bye and thanks to Stevie. I promised that I would stop in at the library over the summer, and she promised to drop by the store.

On our way home, Penelope seemed to talk nonstop. She was always so excited about life and told every story as if it had more meaning than the last. And if she ever caught someone's attention on the street, she called out *Hi there!* and grinned as hard as she could. She truly liked people. All people. And everyone liked her. Even when she wore a ridiculous blue party dress and strolled down the street swinging her arms next to the tallest, palest, saddest girl in all of Homeport.

Penelope gave me a big hug around my middle when we got to her house. She lived across the street and a few doors down from us, but it was like another world. Her home was practically a mansion. For some reason, I didn't go inside her house too often. She seemed to like being at the bead shop more than being at home. I guess she just got tired of the Gray Moms always babying her. But I knew they did it because they loved her more than anything else on Earth. I wondered what it felt like to be loved that much.

"Man, that was fun!" she said. "Stevie's so cool."

"Yep."

I picked up a pebble that resembled a granite bead we sold in the store.

"So when's your last day of school?" I asked her.

She pulled the loose ribbons out of her hair and started to unlace her party shoes and yank off her socks. I noticed her toenails were painted a pretty bright pink.

"Day after tomorrow."

I threw the pebble down the street. It landed in a gutter.

"Well, have a good summer if I don't see you."

"What are you talking about?" she frowned. "You'll see me."

Next thing I knew, without knowing why, I dropped down onto the mansion's wide top step and buried my head in my arms. The breeze began to pick up, and I felt little drops of rain on the back of my neck.

"Are you okay, Emma?"

Penelope sat down next to me and put her hand on my knee. I didn't know what was wrong with me. All I knew was that I hated my life and didn't know what to do about it.

The rain came down harder, and the wind picked up more speed. But I didn't budge.

"I think we better go inside," said Penelope, tossing her fancy shoes against the door. "It's gonna storm. Do you want to come in?"

"No."

I stayed in the same position. I think I was crying, but it might have been the rain. Or both.

"Emma," Penelope said softly. "Remember when I said I wanted to ask you something the other day?"

I sniffled into my arms.

"Sort of."

"Can I ask it now?"

I shrugged my shoulders. At that moment, I didn't care about anything.

Penelope put her hand on my back and gently patted it, the way the Gray Moms probably patted her back when she was upset.

"Do you think that maybe you're adopted?"

TWELVE

The rain was coming down even stronger now. And the wind was swirling so hard my bun had unraveled. Long stringy pieces of red hair fell against my arms. I lifted my head slowly.

"Adopted?"

"Well, I don't want to brag," said Penelope, "but we adopted kids have a sixth sense about these things. It's always seemed so obvious to me. You don't look or act one ounce like anyone in your family. And I've met them all, from Uncle Spaghetti to Second Cousin Ravioli."

She was right. I didn't have a single thing in common with anyone in the entire Salvoni clan. And there were a ton of them who lived on the north side of Boston. Every Christmas Eve, we all got together at my aunt Lucia's home for dessert and presents. At least forty-five people would be crammed into the first floor of her duplex eating panettonne and cenci and playing dumb games and lighting candles. And the gifts I got, like tubes of lipstick and oversized earrings, were never anything like me. In fact, every year I felt less like I belonged. To top it off, Uncle Raimondo would always holler—*Look everybody! It's the freakin' Frekes!*—as soon as he spotted me. And, of course, Donatella always thought that was hilarious. She would laugh and laugh. . . .

"And let's face it," Penelope continued. "Your mother has never come clean about who your father is. She acts like she doesn't even know. But believe me, women know these things."

That was true too. I never pushed Donatella for biological information because she always changed the subject, making it too awkward to discuss. And once, when I asked Nonno who my father was, he just grinned and told me it was like picking out a piece of linguine in a bowl of fettuccine.

Penelope went on, "And another thing—" But then she paused.

I rubbed my nose and sniffed back tears. "What other thing?"

She shifted a little and wiped the rain off her face with the back of her hand.

"I don't want to say too much."

"Go ahead," I said, "say it."

"Well. Sometimes it seems like—" She hesitated again.

"Like what? Seems like what??"

"That Donatella—"

"Yah?"

Penelope shook her head. "I'm really not sure I should say this, Emma. I don't want to hurt your feelings. You're my best friend."

"I promise," I told her, "*none* of this is hurting my feelings. In fact, it all makes perfect sense."

"Then I guess I'll just say it. . . . " said Penelope and she took a deep breath. "It seems like Donatella may have adopted you just to wait on her and run the store like you're her servant."

I stared straight ahead, my mouth wide open, as if in shock. On some level, I *was* in shock. Rain was blowing against the back of my throat, but I hardly noticed.

"I mean think about it. You work more at the store than she does. And she's practically denying you an education so you'll have to work for *her* the rest of your life. Plus you do most of the housework. Heck, you even had to figure out how to fix that old leaky faucet 'cause she's too cheap to call a plumber! And what about the fact that she doesn't want her boyfriends to know you exist? It just goes on and on and on. All the pieces of the puzzle fit, Emma. . . . She won't even let you call her Mom."

I almost felt as if I had fallen into some sort of trance.

"And my name," I whispered.

Penelope twisted around. "Your name?"

"What kind of person," I wondered aloud, "would name her only child, *Am a Freak*?"

Right then, a powerful explosion of lightning and thunder lit up the skies. It jolted me straight out of my daze. We grabbed each other and screamed.

And just as quickly as it started, the rain stopped. The clouds parted. The wind died down. The sun peeked through and (as if I had willed it) cast a faint rainbow from one end of the port to the other.

"Penelope!" I said, practically leaping up and down with excitement. "If this is really true, where do you think I'm from?"

"Well, I've given that some thought too," she said. We were both dripping wet but neither of us cared.

"I'm guessing Russia."

"Wow. Russia?"

"Or maybe, Poland."

"Wow. Poland?"

"Finland's another possibility."

"Wow. Finland?"

"Definitely one of those eastern, Baltic, tall, pale countries."

It was as if I could see the European horizon on the other side of the ocean. And that other land and that other life were calling to me.

"Emma!" said Penelope, shaking me out of my spell.

"What?"

"It's time you sat down and had a tell-all with Donatella," she said firmly, pointing at my nose. "I think she's got some explaining to do."

The bead shop was open, but no one was there. I wasn't surprised. Donatella often left it vacant to run upstairs and eat a snack or to watch a certain TV program. She left a pair of cymbals on the counter for customers to bang if they needed assistance.

I climbed up the narrow steps to our apartment. I opened the door and stood frozen staring in. Leftover rain from my wet clothes dripped on the floor. Nonno and Eggplant were directly in front of me asleep on the brown plaid recliner.

"Helllllooo? Is that you, Emma?" Donatella called from the bathroom. The door was cracked slightly, and I could see the colors of her clothes blinking across the small space.

"Listen! I have an early date with Antonio, and by the way, he's a dreamboat!"

Nonno was awake now and staring at me.

"You wet?"

I swallowed hard and nodded.

"You sick?" he asked.

Eggplant lifted her head and stared at me too.

I shook my head no.

"So what wrong, Emma-roni?"

I looked past him and over at the bathroom.

"Everything," I said.

"Oh no-no-no-no," he groaned and lifted Eggplant down to the floor. "You got the woman *problema*, we walk."

He shoved the leash over his dog's head, picked up his cane, and grabbed an umbrella. I was pushed out of their way as they hurried through the door and down the stairs.

"AACK!" Donatella shrieked. "What are you doing getting water and muck all over my virtual Persian rug?"

She pulled at her hair with both hands, then ran back into the bathroom to get a towel.

"Here!" she yelled throwing it at me. "Go change your clothes. Then clean up this mess. I gotta run!"

But I didn't move.

She whipped around and crossed her arms.

"Earth to Emma! Did you hear me?"

"I need to talk to you, Donatella."

"And by the way—" she said as she rushed over to the gold mirror to make some last-minute corrections to her hair, "Nonno is going to want to eat when he gets back, so boil some penne for the two of you. There's white sauce in the cabinet. And make him an arugula salad with the canned prunes. I think he's plugged up again."

I gently lowered myself down on to the sofa.

"I have to talk to you now, Donatella."

"Well, it'll just have to wait!"

I raised my voice.

"It. Can't. Wait."

My mother slowly spun around. I finally had her attention. She didn't seem to notice now that my wet pants were soaking through her precious couch cushions.

"What do you mean? Are you in trouble?"

"No."

"Did you shoplift? Trespass? Smoke?"

"Nothing like that."

I folded my hands in my lap.

"Then what is it?" she cried throwing her arms up in the air.

"It's something I should have discussed with you a long time ago."

"Good goddess, Emma, I have a date with a gorgeous, thirty-nine-year-old lobsterman in six minutes! *Out with it!*"

For the first time in my life, I studied her puffy, pouty lips and her pudgy button nose and those large, glittering eyes gathered at the center of her full face that reflected nothing—absolutely nothing—of me.

"Am I adopted?"

T H I R T E E N

At first she was still and completely silent.

Then she collapsed over the back of the couch bursting into deep laughter, laughing harder than I had ever heard her laugh. She was even snorting. Finally, she ran to the bathroom because she thought she might "explode."

A minute later, the toilet flushed and Donatella reappeared, wiping away laughing tears from her face with a tissue.

"Oh look at me," she said, still hiccupping with the giggles, "my face is a mess."

"So?" I asked waiting for an answer. "Am I?"

Donatella wandered over to the rocking chair and sat on the edge.

"Are you kidding? Is that what this is all about? Do you really think I adopted you and never told you?"

That's when I confessed everything that proved it: the physical differences, the total lack of affection or motherly interest, the daughter denial to her boyfriends, the endless chores and work hours, the overall neglect . . . and above all, my hideous, humiliating, horrifying name.

Her giggles quickly faded into a single, bewildered expression as I informed her of everything she had ever done wrong. I had never seen Donatella look so sad and realized I had said more than I meant to say. Immediately, I worried she would lock herself up for three days again. Or maybe longer.

But instead, she scooted the rocking chair close to me and took my hand. Something she hadn't done in a long, long time.

"All these years, I thought I was treating you like an equal, Emma. I wanted to give you lots and lots of space to be your own person and to always be able to take care of yourself. And I wanted you to feel you could be whoever *you* wanted to be. Something I yearned for growing up but never had. My own mother was so suffocating and over-protective and judgmental and paranoid and strict that I was absolutely miserable!"

Donatella pounded her chest with her fist as if she were a teenager again trying to explain her feelings to the whole world.

"WHY do you think I ran off and got married at sixteen?"

"But you make me do so much around here," I protested.

"Because you seem to enjoy it!" she practically shrieked. "The only time I see you smile is when you're working down in the store!"

"Well, what about my name?"

"What about it? I love the name Emma. Everyone does! It's the most popular name in America."

"That's not what I mean!"

"Honestly," she said as she scrunched up her face, "you're not making any sense."

I gave up. It was like talking to a yo-yo.

"So you're saying that I'm really and truly *not* adopted?"

She squeezed my hand and shook her head no.

"You're *really* my mother? And the Salvonis are *really* my family?"

"Sorry, kid."

How could this be possible? Especially when everything Penelope had said made so much sense. Now my life seemed even worse than before.

All of a sudden, Donatella jumped up and snapped her fingers.

"Hold your horoscope, Emma! I do have something that just might interest you. I forgot all about it."

She crossed over to the giant basket in the kitchen where we stored bills and began rifling through the thick pile of papers. Then she found it—a large white envelope—and handed it to me.

"This came special delivery this morning. Funny coincidence now that I think about it."

I studied the fancy handwriting. It looked like it might have been written with an old-fashioned quill pen. The envelope was addressed to *The Descendants of Boris Horace Freke.*

"But we're not descendants of Boris Horace anybody," I said, adding, "was he really named Boris Horace?"

Donatella nudged me. "Just open it already."

Inside was a piece of mint-colored stationery lined in tiny clumps of trees.

Please join us
for the 59th Annual
FREKE FAMILY REUNION
Friday, June 27th—Monday, June 30th
Paul Bunyan State Park and Campground
NEW THULE, Wisconsin

I was confused.

"What has this got to do with me other than the fact that I am forced to share Walter's horrible last name because it's good for business?"

"This happens to be the clan you're looking for," she said casually as she lifted her pocketbook from the coat rack and did one last makeup check in the mirror.

"What is that supposed to mean?"

"I mean, you take after his side of the family. I think you should go and see for yourself."

"But you said I wasn't related to *him*!"

She threw her shawl dramatically across her shoulders and pursed her ruby red lips.

"I never actually *said* that, Emma—I told you we got divorced a year before you were born. You decided to draw your own conclusions."

I stood up, shook the invitation at her, and yelled louder than I ever had in my whole life.

"So what exactly are you telling me, Donatella?!"

My mother paused at the door before she left for her date with the lobsterman. Then she melted into one huge smile as if she were giving me the best news of my life.

"That whether you like it or not, the truth is *honey* . . . you really are a Freke."

When she slammed the door shut, a small burst of wind blew through the apartment. I remained standing and allowed the breeze to swirl around me and through the room.

It's difficult to describe what I was feeling. Other than totally stunned.

I wasn't exactly pleased about this shocking confession (twelve years later than it should have been). But after letting the news sink in, I did feel, I don't know, *lighter*. Everything appeared more focused. The furniture looked less drab, and the room smelled faintly sweeter. Even the grinding noise of our old refrigerator sounded kind of comforting, no longer annoying.

And then it occurred to me. For once in my life, I had hope. . . . hope that I might fit in somewhere and "belong." Even if it was to a bunch of Frekes.

The next week was a whirlwind of preparations. I had just ten days to get ready for the reunion.

Donatella actually helped out by calling the family headquarters listed at the bottom of the letter informing them I would be traveling alone as an "unaccompanied minor." By the end of that day, I had a reservation to fly to Milwaukee, where I would be met by the Welcome Hosts, Jim and Nancy Freke, at the baggage claim area. Already I was excited—these people were organized!

Later, when I asked Donatella if she knew any of the Freke relatives, my mother threw her head back and chuckled extra loudly.

"Are you kidding?" she yapped.

Apparently, she had never met any of Walter's family, other than a sister who stood as a witness at their quickie wedding (but of course, she couldn't remember the sister's name). When I pushed for more ancestral information, Donatella slipped back to her old ways of avoiding the subject. But she did reassure me that Jim and Nancy had to be, at the very least, second or third cousins. She explained that the Frekes were a very tight tribe.

"Believe me, they take care of their own kind. You'll be just fine."

I had one last question I had to ask.

"Will he be there? Walter? My father?"

Donatella shook her head no.

"Even before he divorced me, he had divorced himself from the entire clan. Except for that one strange sister—what's her name? I think it started with an *M* or was it a *V*?"

I wondered if it was truly possible to divorce your family. Maybe someday my mother would tell me the whole story. But for now, discovering the other half of my genetic tree was wonderful enough.

The extremely organized reunion committee had also faxed over a very specific list of supplies I would need for the weekend, which included my own tent and other camping gear.

"But we don't have any of this equipment," I complained to Penelope. She was sitting at our crowded crafts table in the corner, making a beaded ring to sell in the display case. She had finished school the day before, but all of her summer activities didn't get going until the following week.

"Let me see that," she said grabbing the invitation and list of supplies.

Penelope had been even more dumbfounded than I was to discover my nonadoption. In fact, she was so certain that Donatella wasn't telling the truth that she insisted I demand a blood test to prove our genetic connection.

But then I showed her the invitation.

"*To the descendants of Boris Horace Freke*," she read out loud. "So Walter Freke really is your biological dad?"

"Looks like it."

"I wasn't born yesterday, Emma," she said, hands on her hips. "If the man left a full year before Donatella gave birth to you, then how can he be your father?"

My cheeks began to flush. I didn't like talking about any gross sex stuff. "Donatella said he *visited* once after they broke up. But she never told him she had a baby after."

"Why not?!"

"She said she didn't want to complicate things, especially since they were already divorced. She needed to move on."

Penelope wasn't too happy with that answer, but for my sake, she decided to accept defeat. And believe me, she wasn't used to being wrong.

I, on the other hand, was now strangely calm about the whole discovery. I could always tell when Donatella was making up facts or exaggerating a story, but her biological father explanation felt authentic. And the truth was, this boring version of events fit my life. I knew I didn't have exotic roots like Penelope did. It made sense that I was related to people who had annual reunions in a campground in Wisconsin. And I was ready to feel connected to anyone, no matter who they were.

"Hey!" Penelope jumped out of her seat over at the crafts table. "Didn't Stevie say she liked to go camping?"

I had forgotten all about that conversation a few days earlier in the Anchor Café. It seemed a million miles behind me.

"Yep," I said, "in Maine."

"Well Maine's just like Wisconsin," concluded Penelope, "cold at night and miles of trees. I bet she knows exactly where you can get all this junk."

We locked up the shop early and headed over to the library before it closed at five o'clock. As we trotted down Harbor Street, something occurred to me.

"If those kids are there again, Penelope, I don't want to talk to them."

"Which kids?"

"You know, that class that hangs out over in the corner with that teacher guy, Gordon."

Penelope stopped in her tracks.

"But they were really nice!"

"I'm just not interested, ok?"

That wasn't entirely true, because I did want to know what kind of group they were and what they were learning. Plus it did seem like they had fun together. But there was no way I was going to approach them again . . . especially after that awkward introduction when they *almost* laughed at me.

Just then two little girls skipped past us, their mother following behind.

"Hello!" Penelope chirped as usual.

The little girls giggled and waved.

"Hello!" said the mom.

I frowned. I knew Penelope was wondering what was wrong with me, why I was so unfriendly. The problem was people weren't friendly toward me first. Maybe if they were, then I'd be friendlier.

"Emma?"

Penelope stopped again and grabbed hold of my sleeve.

"I just want to say that if you're going all the way to this reunion all by yourself—"

"I *know*," I interrupted her, "I have to be more talkative and outgoing and—"

"No. I was just going to remind you to bring that gold mojo bead I gave you for good luck—you're gonna need it!"

At that moment, I didn't care one bit if she was a little more than two years younger and fifteen inches shorter. Penelope was the best friend ever.

FOURTEEN

As usual, Stevie was sitting at her reference desk near the computers. She was wearing a wide headband that pushed her frizzy yellow hair out at the sides, and every one of her earrings was the sparkly kind. They looked like Hungarian crystals. We sold a lot of those at the shop.

She read my reunion invitation and the accompanying list of supplies.

"You must be so thrilled, Emma!"

At this point, I was more nervous than anything. What if I didn't fit in with the Frekes either? What if no one at the entire reunion liked me or resembled me? I knew if I kept allowing myself to have these thoughts I would probably chicken out. So I put my doubts aside the same way I placed beads in their correct box. Once in a while, I would check to see if they were still there, but for the most part, I tried not to obsess about them.

After all, I was only going to be gone for a few days. Donatella said my flight left Friday morning and that I'd arrive home late Monday afternoon. I planned to stuff my suitcase with snacks in case no one fed me. I also wanted to bring plenty to read if there was nothing for me to do or if no one talked to me. In fact, I had already made one main five-point list for the trip, which listed five sub-lists covering five categories with their own lists:

The Mega-List

1. Activities-to-occupy-myself-if-I-am-completely-rejected LIST
2. Clothes-to-bring-in-case-of-rain-heat-tornado-frost LIST
3. Food-to-pack-for-survival-in-the-wilderness LIST
4. Books-to-check-out-at-the-library-if-no-one-speaks-to-me LIST
5. Ways-to-get-home-if-I-lose-my-plane-ticket LIST

"I have an extra tent," said Stevie. "Do you want to borrow it?"

"Of course she does!" cried Penelope who was beginning to act like she was coming with me. "Can we go get it now?"

Stevie laughed. "Do you mind waiting about ten more minutes until the library closes? I live right around the corner."

"Sure," I said. "Sounds good."

Penelope could barely sit still in her seat. She told me she was going to research everything I needed to know about Wisconsin from the state bird to sports teams.

"I'm only going for a long weekend," I reminded her.

"Emma, don't you get it?" she asked, still wiggling. "These are *your people*!"

I let that sink in for a bit. Could it be true? Would I finally know what it really felt like to belong?

"And you know what else?" she asked.

"What?"

Penelope leaned over and whispered, "You might even find your *joylah*."

"Joylah? Is that an African word?"

"I think it's just a Gray Mom word," said Penelope. "Whenever I'm out of sorts, Cynthia or Katherine always tells me I have to find my joylah, my groove zone, my smooth place back in the track!"

I was pretty sure I had never found my joylah. Ever. Maybe that's what was wrong with me.

"Penelope?"

An older boy stood in front of us, his arms full of books.

"Hey!" she beamed. "You're one of the mosh-pit kids!"

"Yah," he grinned. "You should come back and hang out with us sometime. We meet here all summer."

Penelope sank into her seat as if she had just remembered our conversation earlier.

"Maybe," she mumbled. "I'm kind of busy."

Then he looked directly at me.

"I'm Jared."

I stared down at my lap.

"Didn't Gordon say your name was Emma?"

"Yah, that's her name!" squealed Penelope.

I could feel my cheeks burning. Why did he keep talking?

"You can both join us anytime. We do lots of really cool things."

Penelope kicked me under the table.

"Okay," I barely spoke. "Thanks."

Stevie's apartment was a small cozy cottage connected to a huge brick house owned by a rich man from France who was rarely in town. Her place was very tidy and had lots of little rooms that reminded me of a maze. Everything was so interesting, kind of like a museum. She had a bunch of paintings and antiques everywhere, but all placed perfectly. And she had this wonderful wooden loom that took up more than half of one room.

While Stevie went to look for her extra tent in the storage shed out back, Penelope and I milled around looking at all her cool stuff.

"This is how *my* life is going to be."

Penelope looked confused.

"What's that mean? How's it gonna be?"

I thought about how to put it all into a couple of words. "My own."

In the corner of the kitchen, I discovered stacked cages hiding behind a palm tree. A tiny hammock hung across the top cage. Something was sleeping in it tucked under a tiny red blanket. I stuck my finger inside, and a pointy nose poked out.

Penelope jumped back.

"What the heck is that?"

"That's Cuddle," said Stevie as she walked into the kitchen. And that fella," she nudged at an old towel in the lower cage, "is Puddle. They're ferrets."

Cuddle climbed out from under his blanket after hearing Stevie's voice. He wedged his tiny nose between the bars.

"Cuddle is the outgoing one. Wanna give him a treat?" Stevie asked.

Penelope was a little frightened, but I thought the ferret was adorable. He was so long and thin, like a small weasel, but he was an unusual coffee color with a dusting of chocolate brown and very cuddly looking.

I gave him one of his special liver snacks, which he pulled daintily from my fingers.

Penelope decided she liked him now.

"He's kind of cute! Can we hold him?"

"Maybe later," said Stevie. "This is still his sleepy, mellow time. In a couple hours, he'll get super playful."

I studied the lump under the gray rag in the lower cage.

"What about Puddle?"

"Puddle," sighed Stevie, "prefers to stay under that towel most of the day. It's strange because ferrets are normally very friendly. But he doesn't even like me to pick him up."

Penelope asked, "Why, was someone mean to him?"

"Nope," said Stevie. "They're brothers. I got them both as babies. And the veterinarian says he's perfectly healthy. I guess it's just his nature."

"Man, that stinks," said Penelope.

I peeked in the lower cage and whispered, "I know how you feel, Puddle. You need to find your joylah too."

And the gray towel moved a tiny bit.

The tent and other supplies were piled on Stevie's back porch. She had everything from sleeping bags to lanterns to mosquito netting.

"Can I borrow this?" asked Penelope who was holding a metal popcorn popper, the kind you used over a fire.

"Sure," said Stevie, "if you promise to be extra careful with it. That was my grandfather's popper. When he was a child, that was the only way they cooked popcorn."

Penelope hugged the funny contraption.

"I'll be *super* careful. Anyway, my Gray Moms are old too. They'll know how to use it."

I was overwhelmed by all the equipment. Did I really need all this stuff to sleep outdoors for the weekend? For the hundredth time that day, I began talking myself out of the trip. But then, as if reading my mind, Stevie said I didn't need too many supplies for a quick weekend outing—basically the tent, a good flashlight, and a sleeping bag. She just wanted to show us all her gear for fun.

We spent about an hour learning how to set up the tent and take it down. It was meant for two people, but seemed perfect for one tall one. When I finally got the hang of it and it was time to leave, Penelope refused to get out of the tent. Even though she practically lived in a mansion with everything in the world, she claimed she liked it better than any old house.

Stevie said it was because a tent represented adventures and possibilities, giving you the stars every single night. But a house stayed in one place, safe but always the same.

And that was the very thought I clung to for the rest of the week . . . until I arrived at the airport.

FIFTEEN

"I'm not sure if I'm reading this right, but I think my plane ticket says Departure: 10:11 A.M. *Not* 11:10 A.M.?"

My mother had finally found my ticket stuck between two parking citations at the bottom of her enormous purse. Wrapped in her bubble gum pink silk bathrobe, she was slumped over a strong cup of jasmine tea attempting to wake up before her usual nine o'clock hour. Nonno and Eggplant were already out on their morning walk, which included a coffee with Nonno's ancient friends down at the pier now that the weather was warm.

Donatella limply stuck out her hand.

"Lemme see that."

I had been packed for two days, everything waiting by the door. That morning I awoke before the sunrise at five o'clock and was ready to go by five thirty.

My mother held the ticket out as far as her stubby arms allowed in order to focus on the numbers. Suddenly, she straightened like a soldier at attention. Then she looked at the clock on the wall. It read 8:20.

"My makeup! My clothes!" she hollered as she ran for the bathroom.

I followed her.

"How far is the airport?" I asked.

She was already brushing her teeth.

"Shush der nour."

"What?"

She spit.

"Just under an hour!"

"But I'm supposed to be there like two hours early for security and the whole guardian thing—which means I should have arrived nine minutes ago!"

"Then scoot and let me get ready, already!"

She shut the door in my face.

I knocked on it really hard.

"What now?!" she hollered from inside.

"Skip all that and just get dressed—I'll miss my flight!"

Donatella opened the door a crack. She was brushing her thick dark hair as roughly as you would a horse's tail.

"Just calm your karma, Emma! Believe me, you won't miss a *thing*."

Amazingly, not a single police officer was staking out speeders along the highway as Donatella drove eighty-five miles an hour in Nonno's old burgundy Cadillac all the way to the airport. The car shook so hard I was sure something would fall off.

When the man at the check-in desk asked if I had any baggage—after reprimanding me for being so late—I handed him the sleeping bag and then searched around for the tent.

"Where's Stevie's blue sack?"

Donatella glanced behind herself.

"I thought you had it," she replied.

"I've got my huge, overstuffed backpack and the sleeping bag. What were you carrying?"

My mother giggled. "My purse?"

"Ladies! There's no time to argue," said the check-in man whose pointy face was now scowling at me as if any of this was my fault. I felt like screaming, *I'm only twelve, even though I look twenty, and by the way, my mother is the worst parent ever!*

"It must be in the trunk of the car," Donatella mumbled, chewing on her pinky fingernail.

"Too late," he snapped and studied the computer screen. "Hold on a second. According to your reservation, you're a minor?" He raised his eyebrows and stared at me doubtfully. Why would anyone lie about that?

"Here are my papers."

He looked them over, groaned loudly, called someone on a little radio to meet me at security, and then shoved the packet back in my face.

"Next time, *please* arrive a minimum of ninety minutes early!"

"Well, you see—" began Donatella. But the man cut her off.

"Say your good-byes, madam! Your daughter needs to *sprint*! Now!!"

I whipped around and hurried down the long corridor toward the security line. Donatella had to practically run to keep up with me.

"Don't worry about the tent," she said cheerfully, "you can sleep under a bush or a tree. It's only for a night or two."

"Three nights!" I corrected her without looking back.

"Hey! Pretend you're lost in the woods and build your own shelter!" she suggested brightly.

I stopped and glared.

"Kidding!" she hollered punching me in the arm. "Those Frekes will help you out. Don't you worry one bit!"

How could this be happening? I wondered. Can anything ever go right in my life? As I continued on, I glanced around at the jumble of lines and stores and people and felt totally panicked. But even though I was on the verge of giving up and staying, deep down I knew I *really* had to get as far away from my mother as possible. Besides, maybe the campground rented tents. Donatella had given me extra money for emergencies, and now I definitely intended on using it.

Luckily, the security line was short. My mother leaned on the entrance post, huffing and puffing.

"Now don't forget to call me as soon as you land."

I frowned. "*Don't* forget to pick me up on Monday."

She took a deep breath, reached up and grabbed my cheeks, pinching them way too hard.

"How could I ever forget to pick up my only daughter?"

I had never been on an airplane before. I was surprised how cramped everything was. And it smelled kind of disgusting, like soy sauce and sneakers. My seat was in between a mom with a noisy baby and a guy with long, knotted, dirty blond hair that kept brushing up against my arm. At first the baby was cute, and I smiled at it. But then it got annoying after a while, because it kept wanting my attention and the mother assumed I would grin at it nonstop for the two-hour, twenty-three-minute flight. I envied the messy-haired guy who was listening to music, his seat reclined and his eyes closed.

The time ended up passing pretty quickly between the snacks/drinks and the TV entertainment. And I managed to put Donatella out of my mind. But just as the plane began to descend into Milwaukee and the cabin pressure changed, I remembered that I had nowhere to sleep for the next few days. My housing crisis aggravated by my aching ears made my eyes well up with tears. What was I thinking? It had been scary enough coming on this trip all alone, but now I had no tent. Nowhere to hide. And what if it stormed?

"Mint?" asked the mother.

The baby reached for it first so I had to act like that was really cute before prying it out of its chubby fingers. The wrapper was wet.

"Thanks."

Upon pulling into the gate, a tiny, perky flight attendant leaned over our row.

"Are you *Emma*?" she practically shrieked.

I quickly answered before she could yell my whole lousy name loud enough for the entire plane to hear.

"Yep, that's me! Just Emma!"

"My goodness, you're only twelve!?"

It seemed like every head turned to stare at me. Even the baby.

"Uh-huh," I muttered as I made a big deal of collecting my stuff.

"Well, my name is Dee-Dee! And I've been assigned to accompany you off the plane, hon. I should have checked in with you sooner, but I've just been so darn busy!"

This was not the same flight attendant who had escorted me down to the gate. That woman had barely said two words in the five minutes we were together.

I followed Dee-Dee and the crowd through several doors and down an escalator into the huge baggage claim area where people were standing around anxiously greeting some of us who were arriving.

"So do you see them?!" the tiny flight attendant hollered.

I scanned the waiting faces several times. But no one seemed to resemble a couple who could be named Jim and Nancy Freke. And more important, no one seemed to be looking for me.

"Nope."

We found my sleeping bag on the spinny thing. It was last to arrive and mashed flat. Then we stood around until I no longer recognized people from our plane. The mother and baby had been met first, by two very excited old people, probably grandparents. And the guy with the gross hair kissed a girl (with a mohawk) for about three full minutes before leaving.

Dee-Dee groaned loudly.

"Well, this is a problem!" she complained. "I gotta catch a flight to Salt Lake in fifteen. Follow me, hon!"

She marched me down in her clippy high heels to a circular booth with an information sign. It reminded me of Stevie's reference desk at the library. I sat nervously on the edge of a plastic seat while Dee-Dee talked to the white-haired lady behind the counter. The lady smiled at me a couple times like one of those fake pleasant television grandmothers.

"Come on over here, Emma!" commanded Dee-Dee.

My hands started to tremble a little.

Dee-Dee reached up to squeeze my shoulder.

"Now this is Mrs. Snug! Hang onto your papers, and she'll help you locate your relatives! Okay, hon? I gotta skedaddle!! Stick with Mrs. Snug! Got it?"

"Um—"

But before I could respond, teeny-tiny Dee-Dee tore off on her high heels, tip-tapping back up the corridor. Off to her next plane.

"You poor pumpkin," said Mrs. Snug, clucking her tongue very loudly. "Now I want you to relax and sit back down in your chair. Do you have something to read?"

I obediently showed her my stash of magazines and books, which I had packed in case no one spoke to me all weekend.

"Excellent! Now if someone doesn't come to claim you within twenty minutes, we'll start paging over the intercom. And if that doesn't work, we'll make phone calls. How does that sound?"

The intercom?

"Good, I guess."

"You betcha!"

Then she handed me a bag of granola (the same kind they doled out on the plane) and took the next person in line.

I suppose it made sense to sit still and wait for a while before completely panicking. After all, Jim and Nancy could be caught in traffic or even running late if they were anything like Donatella. I felt around in my backpack for my emergency prepaid cell phone but decided I wouldn't use it to call home quite yet. Not until I knew if I still had a ride to the reunion.

Instead, I pulled out my brand-new book of crossword puzzles and began on page one, which was titled "What's for Dinner?" Since I did most of the cooking in our house, it wasn't hard. There were words like *ladle*, *sink*, and *spices*. The only one that gave me trouble was 17 Down: *dried bread or tapping crystal*, which was "toast." By the time I solved the second puzzle, "Name That Author," more than twenty minutes had passed. I looked up and, to my horror, saw that Mrs. Snug was gone! Instead, a stern woman wearing a navy blue suit stood in her place, and she seemed to be scolding people with information.

I jumped up and scanned the cavernous airport wondering what to do next. I didn't even know who I was searching for other than two adults with my terrible last name appearing as worried as I was. I must have studied every inch of the enormous lobby, my heart pounding, until I finally admitted the truth.

I had been forgotten.

Even Mrs. Snug had forgotten about me.

I wasn't surprised.

I was pretty forgettable.

After sighing a few times, I realized I had no choice but to get back in line at the information booth. It was pointless to try to call anyone. In fact, Donatella had never given me any of the relatives' phone numbers in case something like this happened. All I could do was beg the mean lady to let me change my return ticket date and fly immediately back home.

As I dug around in my pocket for the piece of paper with my flight information, I found Penelope's good mojo gold bead wedged deeply into the lining. Earlier that morning, when I awoke at five, it was the first thing I remembered to grab. Obviously, I needed all the luck I could get. Plus it reminded me of Penelope who always made me smile and somehow gave me the courage to try things I wouldn't normally do. But right now, the bead didn't seem to be working at all.

"Are you Emma?"

In front of me stood a tall, oldish woman with frizzy gray hair and a wrinkly face. She wore faded jeans and a black T-shirt that read Milwaukee Harley Rally. Scrolly tattoos adorned both skinny, crinkly arms. She looked like one of those senior citizen bikers you see at rest stops on the highway. I stared at her and didn't say a word.

"I'm Wanda," she said in a low voice. "There's been a bit of an accident."

S I X T E E N

"There has?"

Wanda nodded.

"Um. What kind of accident?"

"Rotor come loose on the corn husker this morning," she said, "clipped his forearm. But he's gonna be okay."

I had no idea what she was talking about.

Finally, I asked, "Who's going to be okay?"

"Why, Jim's who."

"You mean Jim and Nancy who were supposed to pick me up?"

All at once, I felt embarrassed, because I was chattering away like I knew these people. But now I was beginning to realize I was entering a forest of strange faces . . . starting with Wanda.

"Nancy doesn't operate the husker, but she's the one taking Jim 'round to the clinic." Wanda spoke in a toneless, mumbly way like her sentences were just one long word. "Looks like they won't be heading north to New Thule this weekend."

I didn't know how to respond to any of this, so we stood and stared some more. I wondered if Wanda was trying to tell me that all plans were off, and I was supposed to get back on the plane. I waited for her to say something else, but instead, Mrs. Snug reappeared.

"Sorry about that, pumpkin! I had to make a dash for the little girl's room." She winked at Wanda. "So are you Emma's temporary guardian?"

Wanda took her hands out of her pockets and mumbled, "There's been a snag in plans. I was called to fetch her."

"Oh my. Is your name listed on the 'unaccompanied minor' form?"

"Doubt it," said Wanda.

"Well, do you know each other?"

"Nope," we replied at the same time.

"Deary, deary, deary," said Mrs. Snug. "Emma, may I see your papers please?"

The three of us stood by the information desk as a bunch of adults in matching blue suits gathered together to decide what to do. Finally, they had me call Donatella.

No one answered, of course. It was the machine: *Did you miss me? I miss you too. Please leave a message or a blessing for Donatella or members of her staff after the sound of the tam-tam gong. Peace!*

That "members of her staff" part always irritated me. I was the only member of her staff.

"She's not there."

Mrs. Snug suggested, "Cell phone?"

"She never has it on," I muttered.

Two scary men, the mean lady, and nice Mrs. Snug all told me to sit down (again) and wait while Wanda showed them every piece of identification in her wallet. Then the next thing I knew, Wanda was on the phone apparently trying to reach Jim and Nancy in the emergency room. My hands were now sweating from trembling so much.

What a mess.

I wondered if these ridiculous things happened to most people, even just a few other people. Or was it just me? It seemed like for every little step forward I took, something or someone pushed me back two gigantic steps. What if my whole life ended up being like this? I'd never get anywhere.

"Emma?" cried Mrs. Snug as she scurried over to me.

"Yah?"

"Good news! We've been able to verify Wanda's story. You're free to go, pumpkin."

"I am?"

"Have a lovely weekend at the reunion!" she cried as she scurried back to the desk and took the next person in line.

I watched as the official adults headed off in different directions. My mind was twirling as Wanda strolled over. She picked up my sleeping bag and swung my heavy backpack over her shoulder.

"Ready, kid?"

I couldn't move. I had been so positive that this would end badly that I had convinced myself I would be flying immediately back to Boston. Now everything was so upside down. And the day was only half over.

Wanda sunk into the chair next to me.

"These obstacles in life," she said slowly, "they're all good."

I turned my head and stared at her.

"They are?"

"Sure they are."

Silence.

"Um. How are they good?"

"Well, just think about all the knots you dealt with today," she replied as she nodded her head. "Now the next time you have a problem, it will be easier to figure out and solve."

I guess that was one way of looking at it.

Wanda stood up, and I followed her toward the glass doors heading outside. From behind she resembled a skinny scarecrow in her old jeans with that messy gray hair sticking straight out. I think she even had a couple pieces of hay tucked behind her ear. I felt a little anxious wondering who this person was exactly. And was this what all the Frekes were like?

"So, are you like a cousin or a close relative?" I asked.

"Pretty much," she mumbled, "but not exactly in a relating way."

What was that supposed to mean? Was she the kind of relative who was actually a family friend but seemed as close as a cousin?

"I'm a cousin too, but I guess I'm related."

Wanda cracked a thin smile. "I can see that."

As we passed an island of pay phones, I realized I should try calling home one more time. Wanda waited by the windows as I turned on my emergency cell phone and dialed. Again, no one answered. I waited for the gong.

"Hi, it's me. I tried calling earlier because everything, as usual with my life, was the opposite of what it should be. Anyway, I'm here but someone else is driving me to the reunion. Her name is Wanda, and she's some kind of cousin. I remembered to call you, Donatella, so remember to pick me up on Monday."

We climbed into Wanda's run-down pickup truck, which was parked on the top floor of the airport garage. The dark vinyl seat was blazing hot from the sun. I had never met a real farmer before, but I was pretty sure that was what Wanda did for a living. Aside from the way she was dressed, there were shovels and boards and wiring in the bed of the truck. And stacked between us on the front seat were a bunch of tattered magazines called *The Corn and Cob*.

After Wanda shoved the gear stick into reverse, we didn't say a word for at least an hour. For one thing, the truck engine was loud. And on top of that, the windows were open since it was such a hot day. Not to mention, Wanda had the radio tuned to some fiddling, square-dancing music, which made it kind of hard to talk at all or even think. I decided to gaze out the window and take in everything I could absorb. After all, it was my first true adventure . . . even if it seemed doomed from the start.

The state of Wisconsin was wide open compared to the East Coast. I liked how everything seemed to be pre-cisely built and organized from the neat rows of houses to the parking lots and malls. Even the trees seemed to be perfectly spaced. Back home nothing matched, and roads wound up and down and all over the place making them hard to follow.

As the city highway faded away and the landscape changed to rolling hills, I realized I had not eaten any-thing all day other than stale bags of airplane granola. My stomach was growling, but you couldn't hear it over all the truck noise. I reached down and opened my backpack just as Wanda swerved off the road.

"Gotta stop for diesel," she said. "Wanna pop, kid?"

"Wanna what?"

She pulled up to the fuel tanks under the dirty old sign that read, Gas 'n' Gulp. When she turned off the truck, it seemed so silent.

"A root beer or something?"

I shrugged my shoulders and replied, "Not really, thank you," which actually meant, *yes, but don't worry about me.*

Wanda climbed out and stretched her arms before picking up the nozzle on the gas tank. I slid out on my side and unwrapped a package of peanut butter crackers from my stash of emergency supplies. I took a bite and glanced around. Across the street was a green field with spotted cows. The sky was bright blue, and the sun was summertime hot, not a cloud around. That's when I figured out what felt so different. The air was still. No wind. And it all smelled like warm, freshly cut grass instead of a damp, salty ocean breeze.

Wanda squinted at me as I munched as quietly as I could. Then she leaned against the truck as she waited for it to fill up.

"You're a real tall sapling," she said. "Just like the rest of them."

That seemed like a strange comment coming from her. Didn't Wanda notice that she was mega-vertical too? In fact, she kind of looked like she could be my grandmother which was weird to think about. I even detected some light red hair framing the edge of her forehead. I started to wonder if she was a real cousin. But if that was the case, then why wouldn't she be related?

"Would you like a cracker?" I asked her.

"A cracker?" she grunted. "That's not food."

The hose clicked off, and Wanda returned the nozzle to the tank. Then she disappeared inside the store to pay for the gas. A few minutes later, she exited holding a cardboard carton with two sodas, two fat sausages covered in melted cheese, and steaming hot curly fries. It all smelled delicious.

With the truck running again and the radio blaring, I gazed back out the window and ate my lunch slowly, savoring every smoky bite. I guess I was hungrier than I thought. Outside the open, hilly landscape grew more wooded as the road changed from two lanes to one.

Silently I played the alphabet game, which I used to do with Nonno when I was younger on the long car rides into Boston to see the Salvonis. The idea is to find something along the highway that starts with each letter of the alphabet. For example, *A* for "ambulance," *B* for "building." (Nonno usually got confused and either skipped randomly through the letters or slipped into Italian.)

The game was much more challenging on a forested, narrow highway winding toward northern Wisconsin. I had just found *R* for "rock" when Wanda switched on the blinker. Up ahead, a wooden sign with carved letters read:

Welcome to
NEW THULE
Paradise of the North

Wanda shifted down a gear.

"One more turn, and we're there," she said.

The reunion—

Somehow I had sort of forgotten about it between the alphabet game and daydreaming. I may have even fallen asleep for a while. All at once, I didn't want the car ride to end. This had been enough of an adventure. I picked up the sleeping bag and hugged it for support as if I were a little kid getting dropped off at some horrible summer camp.

We made our way slowly down a dirt road that barely seemed wide enough for just one car. Wanda had to carefully maneuver around the deep muddy puddles. Just ahead, a sign made from tree logs arched between two enormous pine trees. It read:

PAUL BUNYAN STATE PARK AND CAMPGROUND

My heart began pounding as my stomach clenched with the thought of meeting so many strange people all at once. I had to keep reminding myself that it was just for a few days. I could survive for *just a few days*.

Wanda jammed the truck into park but left the engine running. She peered over at me.

"Have a nice time."

What was she talking about?

"Aren't you staying for the reunion?"

"Nope."

Now I was really anxious. At least there would have been one semifamiliar face.

"But I thought you said you were a cousin?"

"That's right, but I'm not staying."

I focused on the sleeping bag and hugged it harder.

"Can't you visit for a little bit?"

Wanda frowned and stared forward through the windshield. For a family reunion, the place seemed awfully quiet. Not a person in sight. Not even a squirrel.

"Gotta get back and help with chores," she said glancing up at the sun which was below the treetops. "It's gonna be dark in a few hours."

All of a sudden I worried that this was the wrong place. What if she dropped me off in the middle of nowhere at a different Paul Bunyan Campground? How would I last the night all by myself in the woods without a tent?

"Are you sure this is where they're having it?"

I was hoping Wanda would realize that she had made a huge mistake and that the only thing to do was to drive me back to the airport. I no longer felt brave or interested in adventures one tiny bit.

But instead, Wanda opened the ashtray and pulled out a stick of gum.

"They've been having this shindig for over fifty years right here in New Thule." She popped the gum in her mouth and began to chew real slowly, like her teeth might fall out. "Most of the family lives in these parts."

I drooped against my sleeping bag. It had been such a long day already. I couldn't find the strength to get out of the truck. What had I been thinking, doing this all by myself? And how could Donatella let me fly off alone to a bunch of strange relatives she had never even met?

Wanda offered me the shiny silver package. "Want one?"

I took a piece for later and stuck it in my pocket where the gold bead was tucked away. The good luck bead. Again, I was reminded of Penelope. Brave, spirited, try-anything Penelope. She would be so disappointed if I returned to Homeport having chickened out on the reunion.

It was *just for a few days, just for a few days . . .*

I opened the door and stepped out before I changed my mind.

"Thank you for the ride."

Wanda leaned across the seat and cranked the window all the way open.

"These are your folks, kid. Don't fret. They'll take good care of you."

"Then why don't you stay?"

For some reason, I was really beginning to like (or was it trust?) Wanda.

She leaned back in and crunched the gears into reverse.

"'Cause I don't fit the mold."

"What mold?"

"Any mold," she muttered.

"Huh?"

"Just remember this, Emma—not every Jell-O salad turns out perfect. But it can still taste real good."

As she backed the truck slowly down the banged up road, I wondered what Jell-O salad and molds had to do with anything when, suddenly, Wanda braked in the middle of the road and hung her head out the door.

"I'll pick you up Monday in time for your plane. Meet me here!" she hollered, then slammed the door and continued in reverse.

I had never met anyone like Wanda, but I was already missing her and couldn't wait to see her again in three days. Because that would mean I had survived. I gazed wistfully at the truck as it disappeared around the bend . . . and the clatter of the old engine faded away.

SEVENTEEN

About a quarter mile past the huge arching sign, I saw my first hint of life, a freckled little boy with light orange hair dragging a branch. But before I could ask him any-thing, he dropped the stick and raced away from me like I'd shouted *boo!* I wondered if I seemed that scary. At least I knew there had to be other people somewhere back there.

As I turned the last corner, tired and hot from lug-ging my stuff, a log cabin with a bright red roof appeared up ahead through the trees. I could see a crowd of young children gathering and chatting on the front porch. There had to have been at least twenty little kids. Maybe this *was* some horrible summer camp. I didn't know what to do, so I stopped cold. I dreaded these social situations so much. Would I have to tell them my name and hear them all laugh?

Then I remembered—maybe they all had the same awful last name as I did!

I moved forward staring down at the ground. Hopefully they wouldn't notice me. I practically tiptoed the rest of the way until I passed the cabin. All at once, it was quiet. I peered up. Every pale, young face was staring back at me. The shy little boy I had seen earlier stepped forward.

"Are you Emma?"

I was so relieved. They knew who I was so they *had* to be related. I tried my hardest to smile nice and wide as I announced my name to a bunch of kids who wouldn't laugh for once.

"Yep, I'm Emma *Freke!*"

At first it felt great to say that out loud. But their faces dropped like I had said something wrong. Then a few kids actually began to giggle. More and more joined in until they were all laughing so hard they tumbled down the porch steps and ran off into the woods clutching their sides.

I didn't understand what had just happened. Could it be a different family reunion waiting for a different Emma? Or perhaps they weren't laughing at my name at all—what if they were laughing at me?

Out of nowhere, a kid dropped out of a tree a few feet in front of me. He was an older boy, darker than all the other children, but not much taller than them. His black hair was wavy, and he had these big ears, shaped like teacups. He hopped forward and stood directly in front of my face looking up. He was several inches shorter than me, but I could tell from the brown fuzz on his chin that he was probably older. My cheeks were burning with embarrassment.

"Where are you from exactly?" he wanted to know. His expressions were stretchy when he spoke, bigger than normal. And those ears, probably the largest I had ever seen, moved when he spoke.

"About an hour north of Boston," I replied.

I refused to look straight at him. He was definitely standing way too close.

"So is that how they talk there?"

Now his face was screwed up like I was speaking a strange language. Were they laughing at the way I talked?

"I don't know what you mean."

The boy crossed his arms and studied me for a few seconds. Then he began circling as if interrogating me on a witness stand.

"Are you here for the family reunion?"

I glanced around and accidentally met his eyes, which were a very deep green.

"Well I thought so, but now I'm not so sure."

"Why else would you be here?" he shot back.

"I don't know—"

"You don't know?" he repeated and threw his head back like he was onstage or in a movie or something.

I wanted to turn around and tear after Wanda, even if I never caught up to her. But I knew that was crazy, so instead I focused on my sneakers.

"I got an invitation in the mail."

"Ah! A descendant of Boris Horace, our founding family father?"

"Uh-huh!"

All at once, his shoulders dropped.

"Sign-in table is through that door," he sighed as if he had never been so bored in his life. Then he spun and ran off into the woods leaping over bushes and dodging trees.

What a peculiar kid, I thought to myself.

I turned around and squinted up at the sign on the porch door of the cabin:

The 59th Annual
Freke Family Reunion
HEADQUARTERS

It appeared to be the right place?

I climbed the stairs very carefully, as if one of the steps might break without warning and I would fall into a pit of unwanted cousins. I had felt this was my last chance to feel like I belonged, but I was off to a pretty terrible start. I dug into my pocket and found the gold bead.

Just a few days, just a few days . . .

Inside, a tall, hefty woman with a square, wrinkly face and thick glasses was moving importantly around the room unpacking boxes and making neat piles. She wore those old-fashioned plaid Bermuda shorts, the waist squeezing just below her bulging rib cage, accented by a giant fanny pack. Her short hair was dyed a funny pinkish red color and had a white stripe down the middle part. A large wooden whistle hung around her neck. She wore a name tag that read, Hello! My name is PAT.

I liked the efficient, orderly way Pat worked, which reminded me of sorting beads at the store.

She turned and smiled extra wide.

"May I help you, young gal?"

"Um. I'm Emma Freke? And I'm here for the Freke Family Reunion?"

The same wave of shock washed over her expression. Did I really sound that strange? Maybe Nonno's Italian accent had affected the way I spoke.

She leaned forward and beckoned me with her finger to come closer. I leaned against the sign-in table as she whispered into my ear.

"*Frecky. Rhymes with Becky.*"

I pulled back and glanced around the room. Was this some secret family code? Did Donatella forget to give me the password?

"*Frecky?*" I repeated.

She grinned hard and said out loud, "Now you're talking!" Then she smoothed the front of her sleeveless yellow blouse and whispered again, "We don't say the other."

"The other what?" I asked.

She put a finger to her lips, telling me to shush.

I peered behind me. No one was around. I scrunched up my eyebrows in total confusion, but Pat turned back and continued to unpack boxes. I wasn't sure what to do next. I skimmed all the various sign-up sheets from a badminton round-robin to storytelling by the bonfire. It all seemed so . . . *sociable.*

Then Pat twisted forward again and cried out, "Well, hello there! Are you here for the Annual *Frecky* Family Reunion?"

So that was it! They didn't pronounce our weird last name, *Freak*. Instead, they said *Frecky.* That's why all the kids had laughed. Did that mean my whole name was actually Am a *Frecky?* I was shocked. Could it be true that Donatella had us saying it wrong all along? *On purpose?*

"Here is your itinerary for the weekend and your name tag," she continued. "My name is Pat *Frecky*," pointing to her name on her blouse, "and I'm happy to answer any questions you might have, Emma *Frecky.*"

I couldn't speak. I peeled off the label and proudly stuck my new name on my shirt.

Pat tilted her head in a friendly way.

"So you must be our little Emma from back east. Imagine that! We've all been looking forward to meeting you, Emma. Are you tired from your long trip?"

Little Emma? No one had referred to me as "little." Ever.

I nodded my head yes. I was very tired.

"Well then, let's say we get your tent set up so you can rest and then start in on some of our famous *Frecky* fun!"

That's when I found my voice again.

"Oh, um. I forgot my tent. In the car. At the airport. Sorry about that."

"Hmm," said Pat as she drummed her fingers on the tabletop, "now that's a problem. You're going to need a tent. But don't you fret!"

Next thing I knew, she marched outside onto the porch and blew the large whistle hanging from her neck. But it wasn't an ordinary whistle, more like the sound of a screeching bird. Maybe a crow? It seemed like another secret code.

I was beginning to wonder if I could have given a worse first impression. Not only did I leave behind my tent to go camping for a weekend, a pretty essential necessity, but I mispronounced my own last name.

At the same time, I was allowing myself to feel a little excited about this weekend. I sort of liked Pat and had a hunch I might even fit in here. And best of all, I was no longer a *Freak*. . . . I was a *Frecky*!

The door flew open, and the same odd boy with the ears reappeared

"You cawed, Aunt Pat?"

"Well, that's a shocker!" she replied, clearly disappointed to see him. "Never seen *you* help out before, Fred."

"I guess there's always a first for everything!" he chirped.

Fred *Frecky*? I thought to myself. That was almost as bad as *Am a Freak*.

"Well, better than no one I guess. This is your cousin, Emma. She's from back east, and she's tuckered out!"

"Greetings, Emma from the East!" he exclaimed, as if we hadn't met minutes earlier.

"Now listen, Fred," she began, "the first thing is, find Emma an extra tent. And then, secondly, help her set it up at campsite D11. Got it?"

For no reason at all, I felt myself blushing again. I couldn't believe what I was hearing. It sounded like I would be spending hours with this boy, Fred. I couldn't even make myself look at him let alone set up a tent together.

"I'll be fine on my own, Miss—" I didn't know what to call her.

"Good gracious—just call me Aunt Pat like the name tag says. We're all family here!"

Fred asked, "May I take those for you, cousin Emma?" as he lifted my backpack and sleeping bag from the floor.

He was much more polite and calm than he had been just moments ago outside. Even so I grabbed my things right out of his hands. For some reason, I felt like they were all I had in the world, as if they were treasured stuffed animals. I wanted to carry everything myself.

"Fred," said Pat, "why don't you take Emma's itinerary and review the weekend's events as you accompany her down to the lake."

"Be happy to, Captain!" said Fred.

Aunt Pat frowned and waved a finger at him.

"No shenanigans, pal, got it?"

He clicked his heels together and said, "Aye-Aye," as he saluted and marched through the door. Aunt Pat frowned even harder. I quickly covered my mouth so I wouldn't giggle.

"Thank you," I said as I made my way toward the exit.

"Well," she mumbled, "we're just glad you finally decided to come and join the family, Emma. This is where you belong."

Wow. I couldn't believe how great it felt to hear those words.

"Above all, have some good old *Frecky* fun!" she said again as I rushed down the porch stairs to follow Fred. He was still within sight down a dirt path through the woods, whistling a cheerful tune. I hurried to catch up with him.

"How old are you, Emma from the East?" he asked.

"Twelve."

"I, as well!"

I was surprised. He looked more mature (and definitely more confident) than the boys back in middle school.

He twisted around and walked backward for a few seconds.

"Do you and your folks camp much back east?"

I smiled to myself imagining what it would be like to camp outdoors with Donatella.

"Actually, this is my first time."

"Ah-hah!" Fred yelled out as he twisted forward and jumped over a large fern.

We continued in silence. A couple of times, he picked up a rock and threw it hard at nothing. I wondered why he wasn't reviewing the weekend schedule with me as Aunt

Pat had suggested. Instead, he had folded up the papers and stuffed them in his pocket.

Finally, I got up the nerve to ask a question of my own.

"Do you come to the reunion every year?"

Again, he didn't answer, so I assumed he couldn't hear me. I knew I had a soft voice.

"Um. So do you come to the—"

Suddenly, Fred whipped around and halted in the middle of the trail.

"Rule number one! If you can't say something nice, then say nothing at all."

I stared past him startled by his response. What had I said that didn't sound nice? Was he joking again?

He turned back, and we hiked another awkward few minutes without saying a word. My sleeping bag kept catching in low berry bushes so I had a hard time keeping up with him. I probably should have let him carry something. I guess I was just used to doing everything myself.

Finally, we stopped at the top of a hill. Down below in a small valley was a cove at the end of a lake. The shoreline was surrounded by a halo of soft grass. Near the far edges of the cove, dozens of tents were set up evenly spaced. Pockets of adults were talking as kids of all ages ran around. At the center of all the activity, a campfire pit was simmering where a few older grandparents were gathered.

Voices rose from all the different corners, and I felt a coolness in the air flavored by campfire smoke and pine needles. The entire scene had such a dreamy unreal quality.

"Rule number two!" said Fred as he dropped to the crunchy ground and motioned me to join him. "If you want to get along with everybody, always say yes, and always agree, even if you don't."

I wasn't sure if he was teasing some more, so I just nodded my head.

"Good! Rule number three: If you aren't sure of the way things are done, inquire first."

"Like what?"

"Like where to sit or how to roast a marshmallow."

"But why would I ask that?"

"That's what I'm trying to tell you!" said Fred, who was growing impatient or pretending to. "Don't you know there's a right way to do *everything*?"

"There is?"

From his tone of voice, I wasn't convinced Fred actually meant what he was saying. He was still speaking loudly as if performing in front of an audience. But it didn't matter, because something much more amazing was happening as we sat up on that hill. I was hanging out with another kid my age, and we were talking.

"Rule number four: Respond to adults in polite full sentences."

I was pretty much used to speaking to customers that way, so that one wouldn't be too hard for me to remember.

"And rule number five: Never question their authority."

"Who made up these rules?"

"No one literally made them up and wrote them down," he replied as he plucked a stalk of grass and chewed on it. "It's just the way things are."

I was guessing this probably had more to do with Fred and his parents than the whole *Frecky* family. It was hard to imagine that the sweet scene taking place below could be so strict. They all seemed to be having a wonderful time together. In fact, I was feeling strangely drawn toward it when a woman appeared at the bottom of the hill and peered up at us. She waved her arms in a large, smooth arc.

"That's Aunt Molly," said Fred as he stood and brushed off his pants. "She may appear all warm and fuzzy, like old Aunt Pat back there, but never let her or Aunt Pat or any of them think that *you* may think otherwise."

"Huh?"

"Oh and by the way, one last rule."

"Another rule? I hope I can keep them all straight."

"This one is easy," he said. "Rule number six: Don't *ever* tell anyone I told you."

"Told me what?"

"That the rules exist."

"You mean they don't?"

He put out his hand to help me up like a much older boy or a man would do.

"Fred *Frecky!*" the woman called from below. "*Is that you?*"

"They're waiting for you, Emma" Fred mumbled, then sighed. "Ready to meet the tribe?"

And even though it felt completely weird to do, I reached up and took his hand. After all, I wanted to do everything possible to fit in.

EIGHTEEN

By the time I scrambled to the bottom of the hill dragging my stuff, I realized Fred was no longer with me. Just like that, he disappeared. So once again, I stood alone in front of a crowd of strange faces.

"Well, hello there!" said Aunt Molly. "You must be Emma!"

She was wearing the same style of Bermuda shorts that Pat was wearing. In fact, almost all the women were dressed in those high-waisted plaid shorts. And the men too, come to think of it, except they wore a tan version. And of course, a name tag was on each person's shirt, which was very helpful.

"I'm your uncle Ralph," said the tall, plump man standing next to Molly. "What do you know! You've got the Boris Horace hair!" he added cheerfully.

"The-the what?" I stammered.

Aunt Molly stroked my head. "The straight, silky red hair!" she explained. "Everyone hopes to inherit it."

"They do?"

Then another woman wrapped her arm around my shoulder.

"I'm your aunt Barbara."

And then another and another . . . "This is your cousin Kara," and "I'm your aunt Margaret," and "I'm married to your uncle Jordy."

My head was dizzy from so many introductions. I was grateful for the name tags.

"Emma?" a girl's voice rose up softly from behind me. I turned around. She pointed at her name tag.

"I'm Abby."

Abby was slightly taller than me with shoulder-length light brown hair. She had a really nice smile.

"Hi."

"You do have pretty hair," she commented.

"Oh. Um. Thanks."

No one was laughing at me now. In fact, the same little kids from the cabin were tugging on my shirt begging me to play with them. And two identical girls about my age began to unravel my bun in order to braid my hair down my back, just as they were wearing theirs.

"Children, children!" cried Aunt Molly in a sing-song way. "Let's all give Emma a breather, for heaven's sake, and let her settle down in her tent for a bit. She must be extra pooped from her long trip."

"Oh, Mrs. . . . ahhh?"

Everyone giggled at my confusion.

"Just call me Aunt Molly, dear," she corrected gently as she pointed at her name tag.

"Oh, yah. Sorry. Um, Aunt Molly? It turns out I forgot my tent."

"Yes, we already heard all about it."

"You did?"

"Aunt Pat radioed over. A tent should be set up for you over in plot D11 in between my twins here, Morgan and Megan."

I glanced down at my feet and saw that my things were gone, which made me panic a little. Everything was happening so quickly. But before I could say anything, the two identical sisters (who had just restyled my hair) grabbed my hands and yanked me forward sprinting all the way around the cove.

By the time the three of us stopped in a clearing, I was huffing and puffing. I couldn't remember the last time I had run so hard. I leaned over to catch my breath before peering around. Tiny purple wildflowers were blooming across the grass where three tents were tucked under a cluster of snow white birch trees.

"Can you tell which is which?" asked one of the twins.

"Which is which what?" I answered still panting.

"Which of us is Morgan, and which of us is Megan?" asked the other twin.

I studied them for a second not sure if it was a trick question.

"Where are your name tags?"

They both giggled, and the one on the right replied, "We like to make people guess!"

They did look exactly alike with long copper hair, long legs, long arms, long everything. In fact, they looked a lot like me or I looked like them. Except they didn't have freckles, just very white skin. And they were even more plainly dressed than I was if that was possible. They wore matching short-sleeved shirts, light blue shorts to their knees, and flip-flops.

"Is there a way to tell which is which?"

This sent the sisters into fits of laughter practically falling on top of each other. Then they split apart, and each disappeared into her own small tent. I waited for a bit not sure if they were going to reemerge. But I was so tired, I just needed to lie down.

My sleeping bag was already spread out on top of a thick air mattress, and to my relief, my backpack was stowed in the corner. *Who did all this?* I collapsed onto the soft ground and took a wonderful deep breath. It was the most comfortable place I had ever known. My bed back in Homeport was hard and lumpy, and it creaked every time I rolled over.

I was just about to doze off, when one of the twins called from her tent.

"Emma?"

I was so relaxed I couldn't move.

"Yes?" I answered blissfully.

"Wanna play treasure hunt?"

Even I knew we were too old to play stuff like that.

I leaned over on my side and asked, "What do you mean?"

Just then the two girls poked their heads into my tent through the open flap.

"It's really fun!" said the one on the right.

"You tell us to go find anything in the woods," explained the one on the left, "like a berry or a skipping stone, and we'll look for it."

I sat up and stared at their joyful faces. It was hard to believe we were around the same age. Everyone I knew in middle school was either overly moody or totally snobby. These two had the personalities of puppies.

"I'll play if you tell me which is which."

They silently checked with each other first. Then the one on the left said, "I'm Morgan, and if you look closely, I have a chipped tooth, see?"

She smiled hard, and I now noticed the corner of her front left tooth was broken.

"But that won't help me from the back," I pointed out.

The other twin, Megan, replied, "From the back, you can see my hair is a little shorter—it just doesn't grow as long as Morgan's."

They turned around to show me.

"Got it," I said. "Okay, let me think of a few treasures."

"Anything you want or need and we'll find it," claimed Morgan, "promise."

They slipped back out of the tent and waited for my first command. Once again, I was amazed how easy it was to talk with kids my own age here. I reclined back onto my bedding to think about what I wanted them to look for . . . and I realized I didn't want or need a thing.

That's when I heard loud whispering between the twins and someone else.

"You two have to come to dinner now to help set the table."

"But, Abby," replied one of the twins, "we just started treasure hunt."

"It's almost five o'clock," answered Abby. "You know we always eat at five, and you're on the chart."

There was some rustling, and then the voices faded away. I hesitated a second before peeking out. No one was there. I was a little disappointed because I really wanted to get to know Abby. And it didn't make sense. One minute I was swarmed with attention. The next minute, I was abandoned.

But I decided I wouldn't mind some time alone to unpack my backpack and organize my things. I wasn't that hungry anyway. Instead, I pulled out the piece of gum in my pocket that Wanda had given me earlier and felt the gold bead at the same time. Penelope would be so happy—already it seemed to be working!

Not two minutes later, a man with a high voice called cheerfully from outside the tent.

"Knock-knock!"

Then a sweet, motherly voice asked, "Guess who's here?"

They didn't sound familiar. Why did I feel as if I should already know everyone and everything about all these people? Just because I was related to them didn't mean I knew who they were. But in a strange way, I felt as if they already knew me.

I cautiously slid my head outside.

"Um. Hello?"

A gigantically tall man with a rectangular head and bushy hair the color of dandelions grinned down at me. Next to him stood a small woman—well, small for a *Frecky*.

"Is everything okay in there, Emma?" asked the woman. She had very long hair wrapped in a braid and wide brown eyes.

"Ah, yep."

"Settled in then?" asked the man in kind of a squeaky voice.

"Uh-huh." Then I remembered Fred's advice. "I mean, yes, everything is very nice, thank you."

But they continued to smile down at me as if waiting for me to do something, so I stood up. Their name tags read Rose and Herman.

"If you have any questions at all, at *any* time of the day or night," said the woman, "you just feel free to come to either one of us, your aunt Rose or your uncle Herman!"

"My older sister, Pat, has assigned us to keep an extra eye on you," added Herman, "to make sure you have a very pleasurable stay."

"And that you come back every year!" cried Rose.

The two of them were grinning so hard that I couldn't help but grin back.

"Okay. Thanks."

"So, Emma?" asked giant Herman, very gently. "Is there a reason why you aren't able to follow the itinerary so far?"

"The itinerary?"

It was getting totally weird how little I understood, as if this whole family was from a foreign country. Could it be this is what everyone in Wisconsin was like? It occurred to me that maybe I should start writing all this stuff down. What if there was some kind of *Frecky* family quiz at the end of the weekend?

Rose put her hand on my shoulder.

"Didn't Aunt Pat give you a weekend schedule upon arrival?"

Then it dawned on me.

"Oh! I think Fred still has my itinerary."

The two of them looked at each other and rolled their eyes.

"Come with us," said Rose, "we'll trot you down to dinner and give you a quickie overview." Then she whispered. "But first you need to dispose of that gum, dear."

"Oh?" I replied, stopping mid-chew.

"No snacking outside the eating venue," said Herman.

"Or between meals," said Rose.

Herman asked, "And you do have your rammy, Emma?"

"Rammy?"

"Why would she have a rammy?" Rose asked Herman. "Only *Freckys* and mountain climbers use rammies for goodness sake!"

"But, Ro, I thought she was a *Frecky*?"

"It's nothing more than a utensil, Emma," said Rose.

"Actually," said Herman, "it's a lovely little all-in-one device with a fork on one end, a spoon at the other end, and a knife that slides out in the middle! We've been using them for years, long before the mountain climbers."

"It keeps down on all the dishwashing," continued Rose.

Herman added, "Everyone is responsible for his or her own rammy. Even the little munchkins!"

"And I have an extra rammy just for you this weekend," said Rose, patting her pocket. "Now enough of your yammering, Herman, or we'll be late for the welcome toast!"

And since no one else was around to explain what in the world was going on, I spit my gum into the wrapper and followed them down the path.

NINETEEN

"Emma, over here!"

Morgan and Megan waved from one of the dozen picnic tables lined up near the beach. I glanced around and saw that there had to have been close to a hundred *Freckys* sitting down for dinner. The noise and excitement were pretty overwhelming.

"Look, the girls are saving a seat for you," said Rose clapping her hands together. "You're already one of us!"

Herman added, "I'm telling you, those are a bunch of nice girls."

"*She'll be right there, girls!*" yelled Rose.

I was amazed. No one had ever saved me a seat . . . I mean ever.

We got in line at a long table crowded with casserole dishes and plates of steaming summertime food. It all looked delicious.

"Now eat up, Emma," said Rose, "you need to put a little meat on those bones, dear!"

Herman laughed heartily. "She's a *Frecky*, don't cha know, long and lean, a bottomless pipe!"

I glanced around the huge gathering and realized he was right. I really did resemble most everyone else.

After filling my plate with everything from buttery corn on the cob to pork ribs, Rose handed me her extra rammy and a new itinerary.

"Now enjoy getting to know your cousins! We'll chat with you later."

Herman clucked, "And, Emma, don't forget to have some *Frecky* fun!"

Wow, I thought to myself. They were just about the sweetest two people I had ever met.

As I made my way through the crowd, everyone seemed to know me, leaning over to give me a quick welcome pat or cheerful "hello!" Never in my life had I experienced even close to this amount of attention.

The whole table of girls shifted anxiously as I approached. Like all the other relatives, they seemed extra happy to see me.

"Here, Emma, sit here," said the twins who had saved the seat between them. I was glad to see Abby sitting across from us.

"So where do you live, Emma?"

"What grade are you in, Emma?"

"Is this your first visit to Wisconsin, Emma?"

"Who's your best friend, Emma?"

"Do you have any pets, Emma?"

The questions came from every direction. Not only was I the new girl, but I had arrived alone and had traveled farther than anyone could ever remember.

"How come you've never been to a reunion before, Emma?" asked Abby, who had been silent the whole time until now.

"Um. I'm not sure really."

Morgan asked, "Where's the rest of your family?"

"It's kind of a long story."

From another table, Aunt Pat stood up and blew her crow whistle three times, then waved her arms for extra attention.

"Greetings, greetings!" she hollered cheerfully. "Before we start in on dessert—a yummy pineapple Jell-O salad mold—let us raise our glasses to the memory of our beloved patriarch, the one and only Boris Horace *Frecky*."

At that point, we all lifted our plastic cups filled with either whole milk or skim.

"That fiery redhead," she continued, "who traveled all the way from Norway back in 1899 and settled here in the wilds of northern Wisconsin to make a much better—and far richer—life for his grateful and humble offspring."

"To Boris Horace!" we cried out in unison.

"And to our *Frecky* ancestors of the past," Aunt Pat called out even louder, "our *Frecky* cousins of the present, and our *Frecky* descendants of the future!"

"Here, here!" we all hollered and clinked our cups.

It was super exciting. I felt as if I had just joined some secret club.

Uncle Herman stood up next and called out, "Cheers to my big sister, Pat, queen of the *Frecky* family and role model of everything that is decent and honest in the world!"

"To Pat!" we cried back.

Aunt Pat pretended to be embarrassed, but you could tell she was ecstatic.

"I couldn't do it without all of you wonderful, wonderful people!" she insisted, sounding a little like a beauty pageant contestant. "But thank you *sooo much* for the kind compliment. I am truly flattered. Now let's start having some of that famous *Frecky* fun!"

The crowd erupted into applause. And as I gazed upon all my newly discovered relatives, astounded by the warm sense of community and belonging I was already feeling, I couldn't believe Donatella had kept one whole side of my family from me all these years. Obviously, the side I inherited in every way. I also thought about my father, Walter, wondering what it would be like if he were here too.

After the clapping died down, I suddenly noticed something move in the distance up on the hill. I could have sworn I saw a flicker of blue peeking out from behind a tree. I rubbed my eyes for a few seconds, then squinted back up at the woods, but it was gone.

After-dinner activities were listed on the itinerary. First, there was an evening stroll scheduled to work off our meal. Then there was either volleyball or badminton, both played with giant slow beach balls so anyone could participate. Next, it was a family swim followed by pajamas at the enormous bonfire, where stories were told as marshmallows were roasted on special extra-long forks.

"Tell us the story of Great-Granddad and the bear, Aunt Pat," called out one of the kids.

Aunt Pat waved her marshmallow fork in the air over the glowing fire. The shadow resembled a pitchfork.

"Oh, you don't want to hear that," she replied extra loudly.

"Yes, we do!" the crowd cried out at once.

"Ok then, settle down, settle down," she said as she hoisted herself up from a foldable camping chair.

"When Boris Horace, rest his soul, journeyed over from the Old Country, he had never seen such wild animals like the ones we have here. He was amazed by every critter, big and small. But the one he admired most of all was the one who almost ate him alive . . . a frothing, fifteen-foot giant! Who here can identify the beast?"

All the children shrieked at once, "A grizzly bear!!"

"Correct!" Aunt Pat hollered back, straightening her fanny pack like it was a holster. "The great North American silvertip!"

A grizzly? I thought to myself. That's funny. Grizzly bears didn't live anywhere near Wisconsin. And the largest ever found was around twelve feet. We had done a whole unit on bears in fifth grade, so I knew Aunt Pat's facts were a little mixed-up.

"Great-Granddad had just stepped off the train in Milwaukee that morning, ready to start his new life. All day he walked north, carrying no more than a change of clothes and a loaf of bread. Finally, by nightfall, he reached the outskirts of New Thule, not far from this very campground."

Huh? It took Wanda and me about two hours to drive from Milwaukee at highway speeds. How could he have walked it all in one day?

"Now, just as Boris Horace stopped off at Ticklers Brook to scoop up a handful of water, who do you think growled low and mean less than a stone's throw away from where he was kneeling?"

"The grizzly bear!" the kids shrieked even louder this time.

"Right again!" she yelled. "But do you think Great-Granddad ran?"

"No!" we all yelled back.

"Of course not, because he was a *Frecky* and *Freckys* never run away from their problems."

At this point, Aunt Pat paused and gazed across the crowd like she was waiting for BH himself to appear in the distance.

"Great-Granddad quickly searched all around until he spotted a tree trunk under a bush," she continued. "And then, as if sensing the human's plan, that old grizzly came charging at Boris Horace with the strength of a hundred men. Let me tell you, that bear was so big, the deep raging brook barely reached his ankles!"

Even though nothing about that last part made any sense, I realized the details didn't seem to matter. All eyes were glued on Aunt Pat.

"And just as that mighty beast was set to lunge upon our fearless founder, Great-Granddad grabbed the log and clobbered the grizzly with one mighty *smack* between the eyes!"

All at once, every *Frecky* was on their feet cheering for Aunt Pat and the impressive skills of our ancestor. And I have to say, it was definitely a good story, even if parts of it seemed confused with the adventures of Paul Bunyon. But I guess what really mattered (more than the facts) was that we were all related to this super brave person. And without him, none of us would be sitting here.

Throughout the entire evening, the twins and Abby had stuck by my side as if assigned to be my personal body-guards, anxious to take care of my every need. Aunt Rose and Uncle Herman observed from afar like proud parents smiling and waving every once in a while. And since the evening had been so structured, yet so fun, I never once worried about all the mega-socializing. To top it off, I didn't stick out like a giraffe among a pack of hyenas like I did at school. Most of the *Frecky* kids were too tall and too skinny just like I was . . . and if you had the Boris Horace red hair, you might as well have considered yourself royalty.

This, I contentedly thought to myself, *this is way more than feeling like I belonged . . . this is how it feels to be incredibly popular!*

Later that night as I lay on top of my cozy sleeping bag, listening to the loons echo one another down on the lake, I realized everything that had been missing from my life was right here at the reunion. As usual, Penelope knew best—these *were* my people. And her good mojo gold bead had given me the courage and luck to find them.

TWENTY

"Wake up!"

Someone was whispering loudly and shaking my tent. I opened my eyes and realized it was very early in the morning. The outdoor light was dim, and the birds were making a racket.

"Emma from the East, I'm coming in!"

"Fred?"

He unzipped the thick double zippers and stuck his head through the flap.

"You ordered room service, Madam?" he whispered loudly.

I sat straight up and stared at him.

"What are you talking about?" I whispered back.

Still grinning, he ducked back out of the tent only to return with a straw picnic basket.

"Thought you might enjoy a little sunrise breakfast!"

I tried to focus.

"Is anyone else up?"

"No," he said, still speaking quietly. "Come on. I want to show you something phenomenon-able."

"Phenome-huh?"

We tiptoed through the woods until we arrived at a huge rock by the water. The top of it was flat, so we climbed on top and ate Fred's breakfast together. Across the far shore, the sun climbed over the horizon between two tall white birch trees, the sky streaking pink and yellow.

"This is my favorite spot on the whole lake. It's the perfect stage. And see, the water is my ocean of adoring fans. Sometimes I climb up here and practice my lines."

"Your lines?" I asked, peering in the basket of food. "What lines?"

"Jokes!" he practically yelled. "I'm practicing to be a stand-up comic for when I, you know, grow up. Figuratively speaking, of course."

"You want to be a comedian? Really?"

I had never heard of anyone who actually considered that to be a real job. But Fred was clearly on a theatrical path in life, and I could already tell he was a bit unusual.

"Absolutely! You won't see me planted in some cubicle or punching numbers on a computer."

He opened the wicker lid and grabbed a handful of berries, tossing them one at a time to catch in his mouth.

"And what about my name, huh? *Fred Frecky?* Could a comic ask for a better name than that?!"

"You mean you like your name?"

He took a gulp of orange juice, then blurted, "Love it! The only thing my parents did right."

That's when it occurred to me that I had no idea which aunt and uncle were his parents. I stared at his short dark legs, his black wavy hair, and those ears. He didn't appear to resemble anyone at the reunion.

"How about you, Emma? Any goals in life?"

Up until now, my one and only goal had been to survive. It's hard to explain, but I constantly felt submerged, like I was partially drowning. I never even thought about the next day, let alone the future.

"Um, well, my mother owns a store, and so I'll probably keep working there, maybe take it over eventually."

"What kind of store?"

"A bead shop. I know that sounds weird but—"

"Weird? That sounds stupendous! Nobody around here would have a store like that."

It hadn't occurred to me that Freke Beads & More would ever sound appealing to anyone. There were all sorts of shops in Homeport, like Now You See It! which sold anything that had to do with optical illusions. And Penelope and I loved Kitty's Korner, a boutique and spa just for cats. I guess I was just used to the beads.

"I do like our store."

I watched Fred as he chose a frosted chocolate muffin and stuffed it into his mouth. Normally I would pick the plainest one to be on the safe side, but for some reason, I chose a sugary muffin covered in nuts.

"Banana pecan," he said.

I paused for a second. "Huh?"

"I just had an idea you'd like banana pecan. I prefer fudgy cinnamon chip, but banana pecan's okay too."

"Yah, I like bananas."

He slapped his leg. "I knew it!"

There was something about Fred that constantly made me smile. He reminded me a little of Penelope.

"So where did you get all this food?" I asked.

"I jogged into town yesterday and bought it at Fancy's Dry Goods and General Store."

"By the way," I said. "Where have you been? It's like you disappeared." In fact, I hadn't seen him since we sat on top of the hill.

He sighed. "It's a long, monotonous story, but the short version is I don't fit in around here," he said. "And they don't care what I do. I'm pretty much invisible."

Wow. I knew how that felt. But Fred, he seemed *so* visible. It was hard imagining people not noticing him.

"Who do you mean by they?" I wanted to know.

"They, as in every single *Frecky*, big and small. Fat and skinny. Loud and quiet. Dumb and smart. "

I giggled, then wondered if that was really true.

"Where's your tent?" I asked.

"I don't sleep here," he replied as he threw more berries into his mouth.

"You don't? Then where do you sleep?"

He pointed toward the woods at the exact same time a cowbell rang in the distance, followed by three faint crow whistles. Fred gathered up the leftovers and slid down the rock.

"What do you know, morning has arrived according to schedule!" he announced, then crowed like a rooster. "Time to get going. Lots to do!"

"I'm guessing this wasn't on the itinerary," I joked as I jumped down to the ground.

Suddenly Fred's lively face turned very sour.

"Do you honestly think spontaneity and creativity are on Aunt Pat's precious *itinerary*?"

Once again, I couldn't tell if he was teasing or not.

"Well, are you coming today?" I asked.

"That would be a big NOPE," he said as he threw his head to the side, "But listen, if anyone pesters you about where you've been, just tell them you were in the bathroom."

"Really? Why would I have to say that? What's wrong with eating breakfast out here?"

"Rule number eight: Never, ever stray from the itinerary with the exception of bodily functions or illness."

I smiled. "I believe you were on rule number seven, plus you said rule number six was the last one."

"Ah-hah!" he smiled back. "So you were paying attention?"

"That's one thing I'm good at," I replied. "Paying attention."

"Then watch this," said Fred as he bowed, pulled a daisy out of his sleeve, tossed it over to me, and ran off into the woods disappearing once again as secretly as he had arrived.

TWENTY - ONE

"Remember now! I can't say it enough! A daily fitness program is excellent for both the body and mind, people!"

Practically all one hundred *Freckys* were down on the beach, hands up in the air, leaning toward our collective left sides and stretching. Aunt Pat, dressed in a bulging mint green sweat suit and matching fanny pack, was leading us in some exercises. They were pretty basic and easy to do but most likely geared toward the tiny kids, the grandparents, and Aunt Pat herself, who was completely out of breath as she tried to talk.

I was standing between one of the twins and Abby, who was smiling and covering her mouth trying not to giggle. She pointed in the direction of one of the older uncles whose middle buttons had popped open revealing rolls of milky white flesh as he attempted to lean and bob.

It occurred to me that I had never done this before with anyone other than Penelope—shared girl signals. Most of the time, the girls at middle school were giggling at me, at the freak that I was. But here at the reunion, I blended perfectly into the crowd.

After a series of leg lifts and bunny hops, Aunt Pat weakly stuck the whistle between her lips and blew one tweet.

"Thank you, folks," she gasped. "Fifteen . . . minutes . . . until . . . boating."

"Fifteen minutes?" squealed Megan. "What do you want to do?"

"Let's go to the Mini Mart!" said Morgan. "I want to buy a net."

I studied Abby and the twins, and all at once, a feeling of belonging warmed my whole body. Anyone back in Homeport who happened to be watching us would have assumed the four of us were sisters. And I couldn't ask for anything better.

I chimed in, "Where's the Mini Mart?"

"It's on the other side of the campground," replied Abby, "but definitely too far to go in just fifteen minutes."

"Now thirteen minutes," corrected Megan pointing to her watch.

"I could show you where I had breakfast this morning," I suggested. "It's just past our tents."

"What are you talking about, Emma?" asked Abby. "We all ate breakfast together just an hour ago."

"I actually had two breakfasts," I confessed mischievously.

All three girls stared at me.

"Huh?" they said at the same time.

A few minutes later, I climbed on top of the flat-topped boulder as Abby, Morgan, and Megan watched from below.

"Fred and I saw the sun come up, and we ate muffins and berries!"

The three of them gawked up at me, then at one another. A piece of leftover muffin was by my foot. I picked it up and showed it to them.

"See? I had banana pecan, and he had fudgy cinnamon chip!"

Morgan threw her hand over her mouth. The other two appeared just as shocked.

"What is it?" I asked.

Then they huddled together and whispered. I jumped down to the ground instantly feeling very left out. I was surprised how quickly those feelings flooded back.

"What's the matter?" I asked.

Abby touched my arm.

"Emma, I'm not sure how to tell you this."

"Just tell her," said Megan.

"Tell me what?"

Abby sighed. "We don't talk to Fred."

I was confused.

"*We* as in the three of you?"

Morgan answered, "*We* as in everybody in the entire family. And probably the whole town for that matter."

"He's totally crazy!" blurted Megan. "Stay away from him, Emma!"

"What?!"

"You two," said Abby, "you're exaggerating."

Had Fred been telling the truth, that no one at all cared about him?

"Well, it's true!" Morgan insisted. "He talks out loud to himself and sleeps in the scary forest and looks like a troll with those ears. No one likes him."

I stared down at my feet and confessed, "I like him."

"But you can't!" said Megan.

"What do you mean, I can't?"

There were a few awkward silent moments when I wasn't sure if I should have asked that. Then Abby turned to the twins and said, "Why don't you two go ahead, and we'll meet you back at the canoes?"

"Okay," Morgan sighed.

"We'll try to save you one," added Megan.

As the sisters took off down the path, I mumbled to Abby, "Are you guys mad at me?"

"No one's mad, Emma—"

"But I don't get what I did wrong. Or why you're all against Fred."

"It's our fault," she said, "and it's hard to explain, but from now on, just try to avoid him even if you *think* you like him."

"Why?"

"Because, that's how everybody feels. He's not like the rest of us. He has very peculiar beliefs."

"Like what?"

Across the lake, Aunt Pat's whistle cawed, back to full volume after her fifteen-minute break. Abby glanced around anxiously.

"I'm not sure, exactly, but it's best to steer clear of him. Okay?" She took my arm and gently pulled me back in the direction of the beach. "Come on, we got to hurry."

"Wait—what happens if I don't steer clear of Fred?"

But Abby either didn't hear me or pretended not to as she ran ahead, making sure to be exactly on time for the next event.

"I'm guessing it's been years since you had a nap time, dear," said Aunt Rose, "but believe me, it's something you never outgrow!"

She was standing next to Uncle Herman who was licking a purple Popsicle. We had all just finished lunch after an hour of canoeing, and now it was time for a half-hour rest in our tents, according to the itinerary.

"I'm not tired at all," I said. "I think I'll just take a walk or something."

In the back of my mind, I was really hoping to bump into Fred. I had about a hundred questions to ask him.

"You see, Emma," said Uncle Herman between licks, "we *all* take a nap."

I looked back and forth between them, their faces expressing as much seriousness as if they were telling me I had to brush my teeth or eat vegetables.

"But I'm wide awake."

Aunt Rose patted my hand.

"It-it has nothing to do with whether or not you're sleepy, dear," she stammered, as if she couldn't explain the logic behind it. Then she added softly, "It's just, well . . . it's what we're all expected to do right now."

"That's a good way of putting it, Ro," said Uncle Herman, slurping up his last purple bite.

Putting what? I thought to myself. Were we all really expected to do the exact same thing at the exact same time around the clock?

A minute later, I was reclined on my sleeping bag in the middle of the day, still wondering why I had to stay there. It was almost funny. Not in a million years would Donatella order me to take a nap. I mean I was practically a teenager. At what point were *Freckys* allowed to make a few of their own decisions?

I reached down into my empty pocket and panicked when I didn't find Penelope's gold bead. But then I remembered—it was in a tiny pouch of my backpack where I had safely stored it the night before. I dug it out and slipped it back into my pocket. Then I smiled to myself thinking about good old Penelope, and I wondered how she would feel about this reunion and whether or not she would have fit in.

I decided it was probably best not to say anything more about Fred to Abby or the twins. It was better to watch and try to figure things out for myself. But I was so confused. Everyone had been so super nice to me. In fact, no one had ever treated me so kindly, other than Penelope, of course, and Stevie. So how could such a loving family completely reject one of their own? Was it some big horrible thing he did?

Then I remembered what Wanda had said, that she was a cousin but not really related. And then there were all the puzzling comments Donatella had made about the *Freckys*, claiming my father had divorced his family. Come to think of it, why hadn't anyone said one word to me about Walter? You would think someone would mention him to me.

All that considering and supposing and sorting out between what was true and what was questionable made me very drowsy. And as it turned out, a nap was exactly what I needed.

TWENTY - TWO

Following an afternoon packed with activities (from crafts to croquet) and a scrumptious dinner (burgers, potato salad, and another tasty fruit Jell-O mold), we watched a movie outside on the beach. Someone had set up a white screen on top of two picnic tables. It felt just like an old-fashioned drive-in theater. We sat on blankets and faced the hill, our backs to the lake. I had my head reclined on Abby's stomach while Abby leaned against Megan's arm and so on . . . a bunch of cousins all cozy and entangled in one another.

The movie was about a family from the 1800s traveling west to settle on new land. I had a feeling it was chosen to teach us another lesson or somehow represent our *Frecky* heritage (like the bear story), but it was pretty corny and mostly inaccurate. For example, I knew horses like the ones shown in the film weren't used to pull wagons cross-country. Oxen or mules normally did the work. And most pioneers couldn't afford more than one wagon—this movie family had three. It was the Hollywood version of the West, not the real thing.

But I didn't care what we were watching. It was wonderful to kick back with everyone outside on a summer night. I was so used to being alone, and here I was, lazing happily among a hundred relatives.

Then I saw it again, only this time it was white. The evening sky was twilight pale, so everything was blurry. Out of the corner of my eye, a white flash wove in and out through the woods up on the hill. I looked at the girls to see if they had noticed, but they were staring drowsily at the film. Squinting hard at the thick forest of shadows, I could now make out the outline of a body leaning against a tree. . . .

Of course! It was Fred.

All at once, I had to see him.

"Um. Gotta go to the bathroom," I whispered as I uncoiled from the knots of arms and legs. "Be right back."

"I'll come with you," said Abby, "It's creepy when it's dark."

I tried not to answer too quickly. "Really, I don't mind. And I'm counting on you to tell me what I missed. I might be gone a bit."

"*Snack?*"

Out of nowhere, Aunt Pat leaned over us offering a tray filled with chips. The girls quietly thanked her as they took a bag and a napkin.

"No, thank you," I whispered. "I'm still full from dinner."

Aunt Pat raised one eyebrow as if she didn't believe me.

"Enjoying the film, gals?"

We all nodded obediently.

"That's just how Great-Granddad traveled around, you know," she said, "horse and buggy!"

I was beginning to wonder why Boris Horace was such a big deal. There had to have been other relatives just as important, like his wife, for instance?

"Need bug spray?" she whispered, holding up a large smelly can.

We shook our heads no.

"Well, then," she added, looking directly at me the same way Ms. Fiddle did at the end of our sessions, "hope you gals *learn* something this evening."

That was when I got a funny inkling that Aunt Pat was keeping an extra eye on me. But why?

I glanced back at the hill and could still see a bit of Fred's white shirt through the branches of a large bush. I waited a safe amount of time until Aunt Pat moved across to the other side of the crowd. Then I gave Abby a short wave and tiptoed in the direction of the bathrooms.

As soon as I crept around to the back of the building, I raced up into the woods. I was hoping to sneak up on Fred, but he saw me coming and jabbed a stick in my direction as if it was a weapon.

"Crossing over to the dark side?" he cackled softly.

I mumbled, "Why are you hiding up here?" and bent down next to him behind the bush.

"I like to be on the end of the aisle, so to speak."

He had a pretty good view of the movie screen through gaps in the branches, but it was difficult to hear the sound. We watched in silence together for a bit, but all I could think about was Fred's lonely situation, choosing to be up here by himself. And that's when I realized how much he reminded me of myself back home. Maybe, like me, he had just given up. I knew how it felt to have everyone and everything constantly against you. It was tiring and hopeless. And it took away all your confidence.

But here, at the reunion, the world had been for me, and all at once, I felt happy in my own skin. Already I was a different person.

"You know, I think you'd like Homeport, where I'm from," I said to Fred.

He turned and stared at me.

"Why is that?"

How could I explain it?

"I just have a feeling you would really fit in there, the way I fit in here."

"I don't think you really do."

"Do what?"

"Fit in here," he said. "I think you think you do, but your thinking is mixed-up."

I thought about that for a second but then remembered I was trying to help Fred.

"Well, you would especially like my best friend, Penelope, and then there's Stevie, who's so nice."

"What makes him so nice?"

I giggled.

"Stevie's a she. She just has a weird name like me."

"What do you mean like you?" he twisted his head to the side. "What's weird about 'Emma'?"

And all at once it came to me . . . absolutely nothing was weird about Emma.

Fred finally confided where he was staying—in an old cabin, about a ten-minute hike through the woods. It was an abandoned hunting shack he had discovered three reunions earlier but had since fixed up. Like most of the *Freckys*, Fred lived down the road in New Thule year-round. So he rode his bike over every chance he got to work on his secret hideaway.

"It's got a working kitchen and furniture and even a woodstove. I'm telling you, I could live there permanently!"

All of a sudden, the music in the film began building up, signaling the story was coming to some dramatic climax. I jumped up realizing a lot of time had passed.

"I better go before Aunt Pat sends out a search committee," I said, remembering the way she looked at me. "But I really want to see this little cabin."

"You do?"

"Um, yah." I found myself blushing again, but luckily it was dark out. "If that's ok?"

"Sure, if you're willing to break rule number ten."

"We're only on rule number eight," I grinned, "but what is it?"

"Never, ever take a risk!" he said, waving his hands as if the woods were on fire. "Always play it safe."

"That's funny."

"What's so funny about that?" Fred asked.

"I was raised to pretty much do the opposite of all of these rules."

Fred smiled ear to ear. "You're right! I think I would like Homeport!"

Below us the *Freckys* sighed in unison, reacting to something in the movie. I knew I better hurry.

"So I'll skip morning exercises," I whispered backing out of the bush, "and meet you after breakfast behind the Hobby Hut."

"Same Bat time, same Bat channel!"

"Huh?"

Fred mumbled, "just an old TV show."

So what if Fred was a bit odd. To me, that made him all the more interesting to be around.

I scurried as silently as I could down the hill and back to our blanket. Abby's eyes were bugged out as if I had been missing for hours.

"Where have you been?" she whispered loudly.

The twins also stared in disbelief.

"Um. I had a stomachache."

"Are you sick?" asked Morgan.

"No, I'm better now. It must've been something I ate at dinner."

Megan leaned over Morgan's legs. "You missed way too much of the movie to catch up now. We'll tell you later."

I glanced at Abby who was still frowning a little and nervously wiggling her foot. I guess she had been really worried. I felt badly lying, but it was starting to feel a little too uptight around here. And everyone seemed so obedient. I wasn't sure I liked this much structure, even if I did fit in. But above all, I didn't like the way they treated Fred.

I peered up at the big screen and saw that the two main characters (a guy wearing a bow tie and a girl in a bonnet) were now sobbing. Their hands clasped together, tears streaming down their tragic faces.

"Is it possible, Josiah, that I shall never see you again?" asked bonnet girl. "Oh why, oh why, do they insist you're not good enough for me?"

"I don't care what they say, Patience," Josiah gasped. "It's up to you to do what's right!"

Patience managed to blubber, *"But how can I know what's right?"*

He leaned down and gently kissed her forehead.

"By following your good and true heart, my darling."

That's when I realized I *had* learned something from this corny movie and the bear story and this entire weekend adventure . . . to believe in myself. Gazing across the herd of cousins, I spotted Aunt Pat holding a tissue to her nose and honking into it loudly. And something told me that wasn't the lesson she had in mind.

TWENTY - THREE

That night I was restless, probably from napping earlier in the day. Not to mention, the *Freckys* all went to bed very early. We had to be in our tents no later than 9:00 P.M. At home I rarely went to bed before midnight during the summer months.

I thought about searching for Fred with my flashlight instead of waiting until morning to meet him. I had so many questions for him. As I lay awake tossing and turning, it occurred to me he might actually know something about my father. And there was so much about the *Freckys* I didn't understand.

But I couldn't just roam around the woods in the dark searching for his little cabin. Plus, I still had that strange feeling I was being watched by Aunt Pat. And then there was Abby. She definitely didn't like the fact that I had been away from the movie so long. She barely glanced in my direction as we folded our blankets and headed back to our separate campsites.

"See you in the morning, Abby," I called as I followed the twins back to our tents.

"Good night," was all she said.

I wished Penelope were here. She would figure it all out in a flash. I had thought of calling her earlier on my emergency cell phone, but there was no signal out in the Wisconsin woods. Why couldn't everyone be like good old Penelope? I thought to myself. She definitely had a good and true heart.

Then I heard a rustling. I grabbed my flashlight and aimed it directly at the flap of my tent just as a note dropped onto the ground. I yanked down the double zippers and shined my flashlight back and forth across the trees. Nothing. Whoever it was—and I had a pretty good idea who—was as quick and camouflaged as a black cat.

I crossed my legs and opened the piece of paper that had been folded precisely eight times and taped shut. But it wasn't at all what I had expected:

Thank you, dear Emma, for showing kindness toward my son.

What?

I turned the paper over and over but found no other information. So Fred really did have at least one parent who cared about him. But who was it? I realized I couldn't show the message to anyone. Abby would be upset to know I was still hanging around Fred, and Fred would probably be embarrassed by a note like that.

At least I knew I wasn't wrong about liking him.

At the end of breakfast, Aunt Pat announced she had pulled a hamstring, so instead of morning exercises, we would take a hike around the lake, led by Aunt Molly and Uncle Ralph. Now it would be even easier for me to sneak away and meet Fred. After all, who would check back over a long line of people marching through the woods?

Abby was still acting a little funny, not exactly like she was mad, more like she was preoccupied. I didn't know if it had to do with my leaving in the middle of the film or if something else was on her mind. All through breakfast, she pushed and dragged her food around her plate, claiming she wasn't hungry.

As I stood in line along with everyone else to drop off my dirty breakfast plate and rinse my rammy, I decided to tell Abby I was going to skip the hike so she wouldn't have more to worry about.

"What do you mean?" she asked. "Where are you going?"

I didn't want to lie again. On the other hand, I knew she may stop talking to me altogether.

"You probably won't like it."

She whispered, "Does it have something to do with Fred?"

"He has this cabin," I tried to explain, "that sounds so cool, and he's been working on it for three years and—"

"I know all about it," she said, "everyone does. It's a creepy shack in the forest, Emma."

"Have you seen it?" I asked.

"Not exactly," she mumbled, crossing her arms, "but that's beside the point."

I lowered my voice. "Actually, that is the point."

Abby frowned. But I had a feeling I was starting to make some sense.

"Anyway," I said, "I kinda need a break from the itinerary. I'll be back before the next activity, I promise."

She grabbed my hand.

"Why are you doing this, Emma?"

"Doing what?"

"Breaking rules."

"What rules?" I asked recalling Fred's list. "Is there a book of rules too?"

"No, it's not like that," Abby sighed. "It's just—"

All at once, heavy drops of rain hit the ground as the skies opened up and poured buckets. We shrieked at the same time and ran for cover along with everyone else to the sheltered kitchen. A minute later, Aunt Pat limped toward us rushing as fast as she could across the wet grass. She was wearing a bright orange poncho and hugging a clipboard to her chest. As soon as she was out of the rain, she blew her whistle three times, which was totally unnecessary since we were all standing right there.

"Listen up, folks!" she called out, huffing and puffing from scrambling through the storm. "A little change in plans due to inclement weather!"

"Ahh," the crowd moaned.

"Settle down," she gestured with her hands. "I checked the shortwave. It's supposed to squall for just about an hour, so let's all spend that time reading in our tents. Then reconvene here for lunch at the originally scheduled time."

One whole hour! I didn't even think twice. But before I could slip away, Aunt Pat grabbed my wrist.

"Stop off at my tent, Emma," she said, grinning a little too hard. "I have a history book on the brave Wisconsin settlers I think you'd enjoy."

I was aware of Abby watching nervously, her foot wiggling all around.

"Thank you, Aunt Pat," I chirped politely, "but I brought plenty to read!"

"I think you'd prefer this," she insisted.

I knew I couldn't refuse her offer.

"It does sound interesting," I replied as she finally released her grip. "I'll be over in a little bit."

And without looking back, I disappeared between two aunts into the mob of cousins, out the back of the kitchen area, and off into the damp woods.

TWENTY - FOUR

By the time I reached the back of the Hobby Hut, there was no sign of Fred. I assumed he must have waited for me and then gave up and left when the rain started. I was surprised how disappointed I felt and wondered if I'd get another chance to sneak away to see his cabin.

A steady cool wind was blowing in from the lake as the rain continued to pour. My clothes were completely drenched. I decided I probably should go back to my tent and change into something warmer, with a stop at Aunt Pat's.

Just then a pine cone, about the size of an egg, landed near my feet.

"Is that you, Emma from the East?"

I looked up. There was Fred sitting on a thick tree branch about ten feet above me.

"Were you waiting long?" I asked.

He swung upside down like a gymnast and dropped to the ground solidly on his feet. Then he brushed his muddy hands on his wet shorts and shook out his soggy hair.

"I knew you'd come eventually."

In the distance, soft thunder rumbled through the sky. I started to shiver.

"The hike was canceled. I have a whole hour!"

"I heard," he said, turning down a new path. "But what I want to know is, what if you *like* trekking in the rain? Huh? But no! You have to go to your tent and read!"

"Or what if you like to read outside in the rain?" I giggled, following close behind.

"Precisely!" he practically yelled, "And suppose you like to sit in your tent on a sunny day and count your toes? What's wrong with that?"

More thunder, only this time a little closer.

"Rule number twelve, Emma! Never sit in your tent on a sunny day and count your toes! Got it?"

I laughed out loud. "It's nine, Fred! We're only on rule number nine."

By the time we arrived at a small A-frame house with the roof slanted all the way to the ground, we were both thoroughly soaked. Fred had to rattle the handle a few times to unlatch the front door.

Inside the one room, there was an oven and a sink in the back right-hand corner, a tattered couch on the opposite side, and a woodstove between the kitchen and bedroom. A square red table with two broken chairs had been placed in the middle of the space and an old ripped-up recliner, similar to Nonno's, was nearby.

"Nobody lives here?" I asked.

"Nope!" Then Fred stared at me awkwardly. "You seem a tad frosty."

I was in fact shaking uncontrollably as the thunder grew louder and the air cooler. My teeth were even chattering. Fred hunted in a few corners before he found some towels and a ragged blanket. He twisted around and mumbled something as he handed them to me.

"What did you say?" I asked as we both dried off. "I didn't hear you."

He stuttered a little, "Nothing, nothing. Just a quick comment."

I glanced beyond him and teased, "Are you talking to someone back there?"

"Oh, not really. Just an invisible crowd I invented. They kinda live with me."

So the girls *were* telling the truth.

"You mean like an imaginary friend?"

"Not exactly. These guys are more like a gang, you know, a bunch of invisible pals."

I peered back and forth across the room and tried not to think about the mean things they had said.

"Where are they now? Your gang?"

Fred shoved his hands in his pockets.

"I told them to take off for a while. They already left. Who knows what trouble they'll cook up in this storm!" he chuckled and smacked his hands together.

"Um. Aren't most people with imaginary friends children, like four-year-olds?"

"Yah, I know. It's more of a habit. I need to run through my lines in front of an audience, so it helps."

"An audience?"

"I have to practice my act every day—to keep it sharp."

"Can I see it?"

"See it? Madam, the morning matinee performance is about to begin! *Please*, take your seat."

I snuggled up in the old recliner, while Fred dragged the two chairs and red table to the side of the room to make space. All at once, a crack of thunder exploded overhead and a giant gust of wind rattled the tiny house.

Fred glared up at the ceiling. "Don't be so impatient!" he yelled at the rain gods, which made me laugh.

Next thing I knew, Fred threw open a blue cooler tucked under the sink and pulled out a carton of eggs.

"Ladies and Gentlemen, girls and boys!"

I glanced at the front door.

"Is the gang back?" I asked.

"No," he whispered, "it's my introduction. Just work with me, Emma."

And for the next however-many minutes or so, I was completely entertained by an amazing juggler who morphed into a crafty magician (and sometimes a funny folksinger), all while telling jokes and stories. Like a one-person talent show! The wind howled as the thunder banged overhead, which seemed to only add to the performance.

Finally, Fred took a deep bow and shouted, "Finis! Thank you, thank you, folks!"

"Wow!" I exclaimed. "You're mega-talented!"

"Honestly?" he asked, grabbing a chair and plopping it down in front of me. "You're not just saying that?"

"I never say stuff like that to anyone," I replied. And it was true.

Fred smiled so hard I could see every tooth in his mouth. Then he slapped his knee and jumped up.

"I knew it! I knew I was good!"

"You're more than good," I added, "you're amazing!"

Fred spun around twice and punched the air.

"Do you have any idea how long I've been waiting for someone to tell me that? Do you?"

I couldn't believe my ears.

"You mean no one has ever seen you do any of this stuff?"

Fred shook his head. "No one other than you and, you know, the gang."

"But why?"

"They all assume I'm crazy. 'Oh that Fred, he's all nuts and no bolts!' People have been saying junk like that for years."

"*Everyone?*"

"Pretty much everyone and everywhere I go."

I knew how that felt—when the world seemed to totally dismiss you no matter what you did or how good you were at something. Nobody cared because you didn't matter. It occurred to me that Fred needed to attend his own far-off family reunion to know that he wasn't crazy or weird or . . . a freak.

"I'm telling you," I said as I stood up and took off the blanket now that I was drier, "you should visit us in Homeport. My mother, Donatella, knows every restaurant and bar owner in town. I bet she could get you into one of those places to perform."

"You mean a real gig?"

I smiled. "I guess so!"

"Hey, are you hungry?" Fred asked.

"Starving!"

We pulled everything he had out of the cooler as we planned his trip back east. It turned out Fred had a lot of money saved from collecting stray golf balls at the local country club and reselling them at Fancy's General Store. He was planning to move to New York City when he turned eighteen but decided he could use some of his savings to visit me first over the holiday break.

We dragged the red table and chairs back to the center of the room and ate tuna-walnut-olive sandwiches made with ranch dressing on sesame-garlic bagels. They were delicious.

"Can I ask you something?"

"Shoot," said Fred.

"Which ones are your parents? I mean, are they here at the reunion?"

"They're here all right, but we keep clear of one another. We just don't see eye to eye, so to speak."

I thought of that note and wondered if his parents would agree.

"I guess you could say I'm the same way with my mother."

Fred took a huge gulp of lemonade, then banged his chest to help it down.

"Speaking of which, where's your father, who I assume is the *Frecky* connection since that's your last name? You keep mentioning your mother but nothing about him."

"That's because I don't know him. We've never met. I never even knew a thing about him until about two weeks ago."

"Are you kidding me?" cried Fred as he stuffed the end of his bagelwich in his mouth. "That's intense! Especially since the *Freckys* track every cousin practically back to the tenth century. Hey, is that why you didn't even know how to pronounce our last name?"

We both burst into laughter remembering my arrival.

"Pretty much. My mother has always said *Freak*. You have no idea how glad I am to switch to *Frecky*."

"I don't know," said Fred. "*Freak* is a pretty fantabulous name. Fred *Freak*!"

I screeched, "*Freak* is a horrible name, believe me!"

"Hmmm . . . it might even be better than Fred *Frecky*!"

I sighed thinking about how wonderful it would be to meet my father since we would obviously have so much in common.

"So it sounds like you've never met him either. I was hoping you might have some information."

"What's his first name?"

"Walter."

"Walter?" he grimaced. "The only Walter I've ever heard of is Wild Wanda's brother, Walter, but he took off years ago.

I was shocked.

"Wild Wanda?"

"Wanda *Frecky*? Really tall, old, skinny, frizzy gray hair, wears only jeans and biker T-shirts."

"Drives a beat-up pickup truck? Works on a farm?"

"That's her," said Fred. "My hero! How do you know Wild Wanda?"

"She drove me here to the reunion. She didn't want to stay, though, something about having to get back to do chores."

Fred snorted with laughter. "Didn't want to stay? Believe me, she would have been run off the campground by an angry *Frecky* mob. She's a bona fide outcast. I'm surprised they had her drive you up!"

"Well, Jim and Nancy *Frecky* were supposed to meet me. But then Jim had some kind of accident—I guess he's okay—so they called Wanda to pick me up. It was a real mess at the airport, but Wanda figured it all out."

Fred stared and shook his head. "Remarkable! I guess Wanda was the only one in the state not attending the reunion so they knew she'd be free to drive you. Still, I'm shocked they asked her over the UPS man. I didn't think anyone talked to Wild Wanda anymore."

"Why? What did she do?"

"It's more about what she didn't do."

I was confused. "What do you mean?"

"I'm telling you, Emma, there are very hard and fast *Frecky* commandments these people live by. They all believe in the exact same thing. And if you don't follow their self-serving path, you're dirt in their eyes. And Wanda, she not only refused to follow the family manual, she was a card-carrying rebel!"

"In what way?"

"You name it, and she did it: quit school, left town at sixteen without contacting anyone for a whole year, traveled the world as a dishwasher on one of those cruise lines, got tattoos, and married and divorced I don't how many times. The list goes on and on."

But those things weren't crimes and working on a cruise ship actually sounded fun. None of it seemed like reason enough to kick a person out of a family.

"What about her brother, Walter?"

"Same kind of stuff I think. Except I heard he's got a real job now and lives in Ohio or someplace like that. But I honestly don't know much about him."

"I wonder if he's the same Walter as my father?"

"Didn't Wanda say anything?"

"Nope, nothing."

In the distance, we heard voices that grew louder as they got closer. Then the door rattled furiously before it crashed open.

A drenched Aunt Pat, still wearing her orange rain poncho, filled the entire doorway. And she was fuming.

"FRED *FRECKY*! YOU'VE *REALLY* CROSSED THE LINE THIS TIME, BUSTER!"

TWENTY - FIVE

She was entirely out of breath, her nostrils flaring like an enraged bull. Uncle Herman and Aunt Rose poked their heads in above and below her, both frowning.

"THAT GIRL," Aunt Pat snarled, "is *our* responsibility, and now *you've* CORRUPTED her!!"

"Corrupted me?" I blurted out. "We were just—"

"NOT ONE WORD!" Aunt Pat hollered. "Headquarters! NOW!"

And with that, she heaved herself around and plowed through Aunt Rose and Uncle Herman practically knocking them over.

The four of us froze, unable to speak. Then Aunt Pat returned and shoved giant Uncle Herman forward all the way into the middle of the room.

"Don't just stand there, *brother*! For once in your life, DO SOMETHING!!"

And with that, she stomped off down the path.

It seemed like we were in major trouble, but Uncle Herman only stared down at his yellow rain slicker, wringing his hands, like he had no idea what to say to us.

Finally, Aunt Rose spoke up.

"Didn't you two hear the terrible storm?"

I looked at Fred, whose head was bent, his hands jammed into his pockets. He sure was different around the adults.

"Yes," I answered for both of us. "But we weren't running around in it. We were in here."

"Well, no one knew that!" said Aunt Rose. "A huge bolt of lightning struck, and an enormous tree branch toppled down and landed deep across your tent, Emma! The twins came running—we were all frantic! Luckily, Aunt Molly is a nurse. But then we realized you weren't even in your tent—"

Uncle Herman finally spoke, "We nearly called the police!"

"That's when Abby told us she was sure you were up here in the cabin. . . . " Her voice trailed off as she looked around the room like she had never seen anything like it.

My brain was dizzy. What was going on? I could go wherever I wanted any time of the day back in Homeport. I realized they were upset about the branch falling, but that was an accident. It's not like I did something terrible. After all, I had told Abby where I was.

"I'm so confused," I replied. "I just don't understand what you're all angry about. I mean, isn't it a good thing I wasn't in the tent?"

"Not really," Fred mumbled, "because you didn't remember the rules, Emma, and you didn't follow the itinerary, which is far worse than being squished by a tree."

His voice cracking, Uncle Herman said, "That's enough of that, young man."

Aunt Rose covered her face. She seemed to be crying all of a sudden. What was going on?

"There, there, Ro," said Uncle Herman as he gave her a squeeze. Since he was so much taller, her head rested against his stomach. "Everyone's safe now, dumpling."

What a bunch of worriers these people were. If they only knew how loose Donatella was, allowing me to go wherever and whenever I wanted.

The next thing I knew, Aunt Rose yanked away from Uncle Herman and shrieked directly at Fred.

"It's NOT true!"

But Fred didn't respond. Instead, he crossed his arms and faced the wall like a little kid.

Now nothing was making sense.

Somehow I found the courage to ask, "What's not true?"

"That I want people *squished*!" she yelled. "I don't want anyone *squished*!"

"Of course, you don't!" said Uncle Herman as he wrapped his arm around Aunt Rose again. "Now, can we all calm down please? Pat is waiting, so let's just get this over with, and we'll sort it all out later."

And like so many other times throughout that weekend, I followed ... not knowing what in the world was going on.

We shuffled up the north path to reunion "headquarters," which was just the little log cabin with the bright red roof where we all signed in. Aunt Pat was already sitting behind the long folding table loudly shuffling papers and looking super serious like she was presiding over a courtroom. Four chairs were lined up across from her, and we took our seats.

"Folks!" began Aunt Pat in a stern voice. Now she was tapping her stack of papers against the table making her appear even more official. "Let me begin by saying that, because of your dangerous antics," she grumbled, pointing at Fred and me, "a bunch of *good* people missed out on a lot of *Frecky* fun this morning."

What dangerous antics? Hanging out in a cabin? And we didn't ruin anyone's *Frecky* fun—the rain did. But more important, why was Aunt Pat in charge of everyone's life around here?

I glanced to my left at Uncle Herman, who was nodding in agreement. Aunt Rose was still sniffling and dabbing her eyes with a tissue. To my right, Fred refused to lift his head. Why were they all just sitting there?

I reached into my pocket to find the gold bead, and that's when I realized that my hands weren't trembling, which they *always* did when anyone was the least bit upset with me. Actually, I was feeling pretty mad and could sense some kind of rage stirring deep down inside of me. I had felt it before—when I would hear a group of girls talking behind my back or when the entire class seemed to snicker every time I was called on by a teacher—but never had it bubbled up like this, as if I might explode.

"Frederick Freeman *Frecky!*" Aunt Pat continued, dropping her papers and throwing her arms up in the air, "I don't know *what* to do with you anymore. I just keep wondering what Great-Granddad Boris Horace would say about all of this. And your poor parents, here, are at the end of their rope!"

Wait a minute. . . . Aunt Rose and Uncle Herman were Fred's parents? And then all at once I saw the resemblance between Fred and his mother. Why hadn't I noticed before? The darker complexion, the wider eyes, and the shorter legs. And even the ears! Hers had been covered up by her hair.

"The second someone new arrives to the family," Aunt Pat hissed, leaning in toward Fred, "you can't leave well enough alone, can you? No, you and your bizarre invisible world have to make every effort to lead them *astray like you!*"

I couldn't believe it. Spunky, opinionated, noisy Fred just sat there, acting ashamed and studying his knees.

"WELL, MISTER?!" cried Aunt Pat. "Do you have anything to say for yourself?"

I turned to Aunt Rose and Uncle Herman completely expecting them to stand up in some way for their son. Even my mother stuck up for me with the school board members in her own weird way. But they just sat there too, staring down. And Aunt Rose was still whimpering.

The small injection of anger I felt earlier was now spreading throughout my entire body. I found myself squeezing the arms of the chair.

"You'll never amount to anything with that attitude, *let me tell you!*" Aunt Pat continued to scold. "No one likes a loner, Fred—you have to be a team member who follows the playbook if you want to succeed in this world!"

"*Excuse me!*" I found myself practically yelling as I shot up and stared down at Aunt Pat.

All four heads swiveled in my direction at the same time.

"Can someone please explain to me what Fred and I did wrong? Because where I come from, people are allowed to make decisions for themselves."

Did I just say that? It was as if it came straight out of Donatella's mouth!

Aunt Pat squinted up at me.

"Sit down, Emma!" she commanded.

All at once, I decided I didn't want to sit down.

"I'll stand, thank you."

Fred was now gawking, his mouth dropped wide open.

"Believe me," Aunt Pat rumbled, "we are well aware where *you* come from, Missy!"

I started to fade a little. "What do you mean?"

Aunt Pat blasted a "Hah!" across the room. "Your mother is—how shall I put it—" she growled, "*infamous* amongst the *Freckys*."

I sunk down in my chair.

"Infamous?"

"When our Walter went against every member of this family and married your mother—" began Aunt Pat, but I cut her off.

"You know my father? Walter *Freak*?"

At the mention of the name Freak, they all cringed, except Fred, who was clearly enjoying this turn of events.

"Know him? I practically raised him!" she roared. "And for your information, your mother is the reason none of us have seen Walter in almost fifteen years!"

"But my mother said—"

Aunt Pat snorted. "What *your* mother said? I don't give a sharp-cheddar cheese wedge what your mother says!" Then she pointed directly at my nose. "The bottom line is, we don't and never will condone that woman's *wacky ways*."

What was going on here? How did she know anything about my family?

"Well, what's wrong with wacky ways?" I asked. "If it makes a person happy and it doesn't hurt anyone and"— I frantically gathered up all my thoughts—"and anyway, my mother may make a lot of mistakes, but she would never tell me what to do every second of the day or how to think or who to like or judge other people just because they look different!"

The room fell silent. Aunt Pat glared at me so hard I thought her eyes would burst out of her head. I couldn't believe my own words. It turns out I really was Donatella's daughter. And now I was going to pay for it.

And then, like a cork that had finally popped, Aunt Rose shot up and jammed her hands on her hips.

"It's about time someone put you in your place, Patricia Anne *Frecky*!"

Fred stood too and raised his left arm.

"Here, here! I vote for Emma to be family tyrant!"

Aunt Pat shoved the table forward and bulleted up-right. "HERMAN!! This is all your fault! You never could keep your own family under control!"

Uncle Herman groaned and rubbed the sides of his head. His voice wobbled, "But Patty—"

"But NOTHING! No more spineless excuses!" yelled Aunt Pat as she crashed through the front door to leave. Then she whipped around one last time and hollered, *"And you're all out of the will!!"*

SLAM! went the screen door.

Aunt Rose rushed over to Fred and hugged him tight. Uncle Herman sighed. I was in shock. Could any of this get any weirder? And exactly what "will" was she talking about?

TWENTY - SIX

Per the itinerary, the entire family was off on a bird-watching expedition, except for the four of us. Aunt Pat had left strict instructions that Fred and I not participate in any "*Frecky* fun" for the rest of the day. Instead, we were to be segregated in separate quarters with his parents on guard duty. But Aunt Rose refused to punish us, even though Uncle Herman was obviously uncomfortable going against his sister's orders.

"It just seems to me, Ro—"

"You listen to me, Herman!" she cried. "Just because Pat's in charge of that horrid Boris Horace trust fund, it doesn't mean she should be allowed to rule our lives. I'm done with living on pins and needles!"

"*A trust fund?*" said Fred.

"What kind of trust fund?" I asked.

"Nothing for children to be concerned about," muttered Uncle Herman. Then he frowned at Aunt Rose.

"So I *get* it," said Fred as he tapped his forehead. "All these years, we've had to put up with *Frecky* this and *Frecky* that just so we can inherit some money?"

"Now son—" said Uncle Herman, but again Aunt Rose cut him off.

"Yes! That's the whole reason, Frederick!"

"But why?"

"Because it's a truckload of cash!" Uncle Herman squeaked. "And as the result of your endless shenanigans and poor academic record, my sister constantly threatens to eliminate us from Great-Granddad's will. And now it looks as if she's done it for good!"

I was still confused. "Why is Aunt Pat in charge of the family money?"

"She was Boris Horace's oldest and most favored great-grandchild," Aunt Rose said with an air of disgust, "so he made her the legal guardian to his entire estate."

"Now, *Ro*," grumbled Uncle Herman, "Patty devoted herself to Great-Granddad until the day he died."

"And she lets us know it every minute of the day!"

Fred's eyes were as big as saucers.

"Wow . . . I never knew *any* of this."

Herman rubbed his forehead nervously.

"Well now you've done it, Ro! Why did you have to go and blurt everything to the children?"

"Because," she said, her voice starting to quiver all over again, "our son needs our support, Herman—not endless criticism and disapproval!"

And with that, she burst into tears and ran off in the direction of their tent. Herman followed close behind.

"Oh no," he whined, "please don't get upset all over again, dumpling."

I looked over at Fred. The corner of his mouth had curled up in delight.

"Now what?" I asked.

And then for no reason at all, we both started to laugh. There was nothing else to do or say. We laughed so hard, we collapsed onto the grass, not noticing Abby standing right in front of us.

"What's so funny?"

"Abby! What are you doing here?" I asked as I wiped my eyes and got up off the ground. Fred, however, continued to chuckle and roll across the lawn. "Aren't you supposed to be on the bird watch?"

Abby glanced down at her feet and jammed her hands into her pockets.

"I skipped it."

"What?" I cried.

Fred instantly stopped rolling.

"Wait a second," he said. "Say that again?"

"Oh, Emma, I was so worried at first when that tree branch fell on your tent! I've been thinking of everything you've been saying over the weekend, and it's really nothing I haven't thought about before. But I realized I really do agree with you. And that I'm tired of being told how to think and what to do and—"

"Join the club!" said Fred as he hopped to his feet. "Say, have you heard that we're all being oppressed by a very large inheritance?"

Abby looked at me. "Huh?"

I smiled and replied, "It's kind of a long story."

That night at our farewell dinner, the twins had about a million questions for us as did the other girls at our table. All sorts of rumors had been spreading, but Abby and I had no idea what we were allowed to say. To make matters worse, the quieter we were, the more curious they became.

Aunt Pat had not left her tent since our confrontation. And because she was furious with Uncle Herman, she put Uncle Ralph, the twins' father, in charge of the farewell speech.

After a final dinner of barbecue chicken, coleslaw, and yet another variety of Jell-O mold, people began clanging their rammies together. It was a family tradition done every time before a toast.

"Our dear cousin Pat is suffering a bit of a setback, this evening," began Uncle Ralph as he stood before the crowd. "So she asked me to say a few parting words."

He peered down at his wife, Aunt Molly, who beamed proudly. Uncle Herman and Aunt Pat sat to their left. The two of them couldn't have appeared more miserable.

"Let me just say that if I could be a member of any other family in all of Wisconsin, I would still choose to be a *Frecky*."

The crowd sighed in agreement.

"There couldn't be a kinder, more caring group of people in the whole state. Heck, the whole Upper Midwest!"

Abby glanced at me, and we rolled our eyes at each other.

"And I just know Great-Granddad Boris Horace is looking down on us from above, bursting with joy in his heart at the legacy he set out to create way back in 1899."

"To Boris Horace!" everyone called out automatically.

I noticed Aunt Rose now had her arms tightly crossed and was moping even more. But Uncle Herman seemed distracted, squinting at something up on the hill.

"And who has more fun than the *Freckys*? Huh? Good ole *Frecky* fun!"

I peered up into the trees to see what Uncle Herman was staring at, but an outbuilding and the flagpole blocked my view.

"So, let us raise a glass to our *Frecky* ancestors of the past, our *Frecky* cousins of the present, and our *Frecky* descendants of the—"

"STOP right there!"

Uncle Herman stood up with his hands in the air.

The crowd gasped.

"Fred?" he called, still staring in the same direction. "Come on down here, son, and join us!"

All one hundred relatives turned to one another and began murmuring wildly. I wanted to say something to Abby, but our entire table was staring at us.

Megan poked me. "Emma! Do you have something to do with this?"

I smiled faintly and shrugged.

"Pardon me, Cousin Herman!" exclaimed Uncle Ralph, "but exactly what is going on? I am in the middle of our traditional farewell speech!"

Everyone gawked as Fred descended from the woods and made his way through the tables toward his parents. From his expression, I couldn't tell if he was happy or totally embarrassed.

"I'll tell you what's going on!" said Uncle Herman as he swung his arm around Fred, who was at least a foot shorter than his father. "Many of you may not know this, but my son, Fred, here, is a very talented young man—"

"Yes, he is!" cried out Aunt Rose as she jumped to her feet and grabbed Fred's free arm.

"I am?" Fred squeaked.

"And, you know what?" Uncle Herman continued, gazing at Aunt Rose. "His mother and I couldn't be more proud of him—"

"Yes, we couldn't!" added Aunt Rose.

"You couldn't?" Fred yelped.

"And if the rest of this family can't be as kind and caring as Cousin Ralph would lead us to believe, well then,"

Uncle Herman paused, "this will have to be our last family reunion."

"Oh, Herman!" gushed Aunt Rose as she stretched across Fred to hug her giant of a husband.

The crowd gasped even louder this time, then broke out into noisy whispers.

"Emma," begged Morgan, "what's this all about?"

"Come on, *please*?" the girls cried.

Abby answered for me. "It's kind of a long story."

And then, as if the turn of events couldn't get more dramatic, Aunt Pat appeared. Her pinkish red hair was smashed on one side of her head as if she had slept on it for three days. The buttons on her blouse were in the wrong holes, and her fanny pack had slipped below her chunky hips.

Now the crowd fell silent as all eyes were on her.

"HERMAN LESLEY *FRECKY*!" roared Aunt Pat. "I've devoted my life to making this fine family what it is today!"

The relatives swiveled their heads to stare back at Uncle Herman.

"No one is arguing with you, Patty," he whined.

Heads turned back to Aunt Pat.

"But you're undermining my authority in this family," she hollered, slurring her words a little, "and that's even worse!"

Heads pivoted again like we were watching a tennis match.

"We just feel everyone should be included, Pat!" cried Aunt Rose holding Fred tight. "And that means *everyone!*"

And that's when Abby, to my amazement, started to clap. So I joined her, and we clapped harder. Then Fred began to clap, as did Uncle Herman and Aunt Rose and then the twins and the rest of the girls at our table. And eventually one by one, everyone started clapping like crazy.

Aunt Pat was so rattled that she picked up the whistle that was twisted around her neck and blew into it over and over again until everyone finally quieted down.

"WHOMEVER," she yelled, "has a problem with the way matters are *conducted* in this family, they can meet with me personally, one-on-one. This will not be open for public debate!"

The murmuring subsided.

"Now! I believe it is time, as is our custom, to light the farewell bonfire! So gather up those dirty dishes," she growled, "rinse your rammies and, *darn it*, get back to some good old-fashioned *Frecky* fun!"

And with that, she whipped around and fell a little off balance before marching back in the direction of her tent. But as soon as she was out of sight, everyone returned to chattering. Abby and I ran over to Fred, and to my surprise, a small crowd had already formed around him. Little kids were pulling at his sleeves, and several of the adults were patting him on the back.

We managed to squeeze into the circle.

"Looks like you may have found an audience!" I said.

Fred laughed. "Yah, maybe the old invisible gang is ready to move on."

"Sorry for the way everyone's treated you, Fred," said Abby.

He nodded and smiled.

Then I dug around in my pocket and pulled out Penelope's gold bead. "Here," I said, handing it to him. "It's for good luck."

"Really?" he asked. "Does it work?"

"It more than works. It's practically magical."

TWENTY - SEVEN

As I laid on my sleeping bag that night thinking about the last two and half days, it dawned on me that maybe Donatella hadn't been a complete disaster as a parent. And that maybe I was more like her than I had realized. In fact, it seemed as if I was half *Frecky* and half *Freak*. So I sat up, pulled out a notebook from my reunion survival kit, and made two lists.

What Makes Me a Frecky?

1. Physical traits
2. Organizational skills
3. Steady disposition
4. Predictability
5. Prefer structure/schedule (but only when it includes my input)

What Makes Me a Freak?

1. Make my own decisions
2. Independent
3. Curious
4. Open-minded
5. Doesn't judge other people (*or* myself) *or* tell them what to do *or* how they should spend every single minute of their lives

A little flashlight swirled across the top of the tent. I unzipped the double flap. It was Abby and Fred.

"Hey you guys!" I whispered loudly. "What are you doing?"

"Come on," said Fred.

I climbed through the hole. "Where are we going?"

"I don't know." Abby shrugged her shoulders. "He wants to show us something,"

The three of us crept through the woods back to Fred's big boulder by the lake. We climbed on top of the flat stage and gazed up at the twinkling sky. There had to have been a bazillion stars. Fred used his small flashlight to project an outline of the constellations.

"That's Ursa Minor, the Little Bear. And over there is Orion the Hunter. And of course, that's the Big Dipper. Do you see which one is the Little Dipper?"

He made the shape of a ladle with the stream of light.

"Yah, I see it," I said, pointing to the middle of the sky.

"The very tip of it is Polaris, the North Star."

"The bright one?" asked Abby.

"Yep," he replied. "So I was thinking that whenever any of us looks up at the sky at night, we should remember to wave hello to the old North Star, because—" he paused, "because maybe all three of us will be looking at it at the same time."

"That's a great idea!" said Abby.

I remembered what Stevie had said, that sleeping outdoors represented adventures and possibilities and gave you the stars every single night. Now I knew it was true.

To the left of the North Star, a brilliant flash streaked across the moon.

Abby and I squealed at the same time, "What was that?"

"Crikey!" replied Fred, "it was a meteor, a shooting star!" Then he added, "You *have to* make a wish when you see one."

Normally, as was the case on my birthday, I didn't believe in wishes. But now things were different, and I actually felt my wish might come true.

I wished that I would always know the way back to my joylah, my groove zone, my back in the smooth track . . . exactly where I was at that very moment.

Since we were all packing and getting ready to go home, breakfast was a quick buffet, only cold stuff like cereal and yogurt.

I had no idea what the mood was usually like when these reunions ended, but this morning everyone seemed so cheerful. Like the weekend was just beginning rather than ending. And I noticed Aunt Pat and her crow whistle were nowhere to be seen or heard. Maybe things would work out for the best after all.

The picnic tables had already been stacked, so Abby, Morgan, Megan, and I sat down by the water to eat. And we finally got a chance to tell the twins the whole story. After all, we figured they'd find out about the trust fund sooner or later.

At first they didn't believe us, but then they finally admitted that it made a lot of sense. Particularly the part about Aunt Pat running everyone's lives.

"Thanks to you, Emma," said Morgan, "a few things will probably change around here."

"Yah," said Megan. "Maybe now we can walk alone to Fancy's General Store and read books we want to read and wear skinny jeans!"

"I wouldn't go that far," Abby laughed. "But they're right, Emma. Because of you, life will definitely get a lot more interesting."

"Gosh," I said. "I've never really made a difference before."

"But I still think Fred's icky," said Megan.

"And those horrible ears!" added Morgan.

"You two have to give him a chance," said Abby. "He's very funny."

"Back in Homeport," I explained, "everyone thinks I'm *icky*. And maybe my ears aren't my worst feature, just a bit droopy, but compared to everyone else, I'm too tall and too pale and my hair is too red and—"

"Emma, what are you talking about?" cried Abby. "You're the prettiest one here!"

The twins nodded in agreement.

"Huh?" was all I could manage to say.

And then I caught a glimpse of my reflection in the lake. Something had changed. I no longer looked like a total freak. In fact, I didn't look half bad.

We dropped off our dirty dishes and rinsed our rammies for the last time. Then we all headed back to our sites to pack. I was surprised, but not really, to find my tent had been dismantled and taken away. My backpack and sleeping bag were tucked under the birch tree.

"When did you do that, Emma?" asked Morgan.

"I didn't."

Megan looked confused. "Then who did?"

"I guess the same mysterious person who set it up when I arrived." I grinned to myself, thinking this was probably Fred's way of saying so long.

As I gazed around and studied the cozy meadow, slightly smashed from all our stuff, I wondered if I would ever come back again. I hoped so. I now had a very warm place in my heart for Wisconsin and, especially, New Thule.

"Walk you out?"

Abby was standing under the birch tree holding my sleeping bag, smiling as always.

I gave the twins a big hug, and we promised to keep in touch. And as Abby and I strolled through the campground, I hugged all the aunts, uncles, and cousins goodbye, thanking them for so much *Frecky* fun.

"Emma!"

Aunt Rose and Uncle Herman raced across the beach.

"You can't leave us without saying good-bye, dear," said Aunt Rose, wrapping her arms around me.

"And don't forget to write once in a while," added Uncle Herman.

"Promise."

Then I remembered the rammy and pulled it out of my back pocket.

Aunt Rose insisted, "Keep it as a souvenir. And you never know when you might go mountain climbing!"

"Better yet, Ro, she can bring it back next year!" said Uncle Herman.

"Oh, you're absolutely right, Herman!"

Then I asked, "Will *you* be here next year?"

They stared at each other all goofy and replied, "Of course we will!"

We all hugged one last time. Then as Abby and I turned to leave, Aunt Rose caught my arm.

"Please tell your mother that *I think* she did a wonderful job raising you, Emma."

Wow. I never ever thought I'd hear someone say those words.

"Thanks," I replied. "I will."

"And, Emma?" said Uncle Herman. "Cousin Walter was a good man. He was just dealt a bad hand."

A bad hand? But before I could ask what that meant, Aunt Rose pecked me on the cheek and they scurried off.

Abby and I took the shortcut up the embankment and followed the trail back to the campground entrance. When the log cabin with the bright red roof came into view, Abby grabbed my wrist.

"Are you ready to face Aunt Pat?"

"*What?*" I asked. "Is she in there?"

Abby shrugged her shoulders. "She checks us in, and she checks us out. I thought it would be easier for you if we faced her together."

That's when I realized I now had two very best friends in the world.

"Do you think I should apologize or something?" I asked.

"For what?"

"I don't know," I said. "It just seems like the right thing to do."

We held hands as we climbed the steps to the porch. I took a deep breath and went in first with Abby close behind. Aunt Pat was in there all right, her back to the door. She barely glanced at us over her shoulder, then returned to packing boxes as if we were invisible.

And that's when I decided, then and there, that no one would treat me like I was invisible ever again. I took another deep breath.

"Thank you for inviting me!" I blurted too loudly. "I had a very good time."

Aunt Pat stopped what she was doing, turned around slowly, and then plunked her hands on her thick waist.

"You did, did you?"

"Yep. I mean, yes, I did!"

Aunt Pat's eyes traveled around the room like she was tracking a wasp. I had no idea what she would say next, but I decided sticking to basic manners was the way to go.

"Do you have anything else to add?"

I realized Aunt Pat was expecting me to apologize and take the blame for the turn of events. But I knew now that I hadn't done anything wrong. So instead, I spoke from my good and true heart.

"Well, it was very nice to finally meet my father's side of the family. And when I meet him someday, I'll let him know what a terrific time I had."

Aunt Pat dropped her hands and grunted. Then she flipped hastily through her pile of powder blue T-shirts and grabbed two.

"Here!" she said, frowning. "You can take your commemorative reunion shirt now, Abby—but don't try to sneak out with a second one when you leave with your folks!"

Abby slipped out from behind me and said, "Thank you!"

"And here's yours," she said to me, shoving the shirt under my chin.

"This is great! Thanks."

As we turned to go, Aunt Pat cleared her throat. "Emma?"

I twirled around. "Yes?"

She rolled her eyes and gritted her teeth, then mumbled, "Have a safe trip back."

I smiled as hard as I could. "I will!"

"And next year," she grumbled, "bring that father of yours with you. Okay? Don't know why everybody can't just get along!"

TWENTY-EIGHT

Abby and I left the cabin holding in our giggles like confetti about to explode. As soon as we stepped off the porch we ran laughing hysterically all the way down the path to the entrance where I was to meet Wanda. When we reached the huge arching PAUL BUNYAN STATE PARK AND CAMPGROUND sign, we were still screeching with delight, clutching our aching sides.

All of a sudden, a body leaped out of the woods scaring us half to death.

"RrrraaRR!"

We screamed, "FRED!" and fell down to the driveway, dropping all my stuff in the dirt.

I wrapped my arms around my stomach because it hurt so much from laughing and gasping and shrieking. Abby sat up first and dusted off her clothes.

"Why were you hiding like that?!" she scolded him, playfully.

"Rule number thirteen," Fred replied, "never skip an opportunity to scare your cousins half to death!"

Then he reached down and offered me his hand, just as he had when we were sitting on the hill Friday afternoon.

I glared at him, but he knew I was joking.

"You were on rule number ten?" I corrected one last time. "I didn't think I'd get to see you again."

"Are you crazy?" he cried. "And miss a chance to meet the one and only Wild Wanda?"

Right then the old pickup truck clickety-clacked down the bumpy road toward us. I had such mixed feelings about leaving, but I was really glad to see Wanda again, especially since now I knew we were most likely closely related. Plus, I had a ton of questions to ask her.

"Okay," said Fred, "love the truck."

"Yikes," said Abby. "It's so dirty and beat-up."

Wanda parked in a little turnoff and then kicked open the driver's door, which looked as if it might snap off.

"Oh yah!" said Fred. "Love the attitude."

Abby looked at me and rolled her eyes.

Finally, Wanda walked toward us, sauntering like an outlaw arriving in a new town. She was wearing the same black short-sleeve Harley T-shirt and jeans. Her gray hair stuck straight out, and she was holding a can of "pop".

"And definitely love the look." Fred whispered and sighed, "My hero."

I jabbed him in the ribs with my elbow and stepped forward.

"Hi, Wanda!"

"Ready?" was all she said at first.

I picked up my sleeping bag, and Abby grabbed my backpack. Fred stuck out his hand.

"Hello, Aunt Wanda," he beamed. "Fred *Frecky*. Thrilled to finally meet you in person."

Wanda raised one eyebrow suspiciously, then carefully shook his hand.

"You can drop the Aunt bit. Wanda's fine."

"Wanda, this is Abby," I said.

Wanda nodded her head. "You kids had a good weekend?"

"Interesting," commented Fred, "to say the least."

Wanda took my backpack from Abby and studied me. "Looks like you survived."

And then, out of nowhere, I burst into tears like a baby. I had more than survived. I felt like a new person. And I really didn't want to say good-bye to Abby and Fred!

"Are you okay, Emma?" asked Abby. She patted my back, the same way Penelope had on the porch steps, which made me cry even harder.

"I'm going to miss you guys SO MUCH!"

"Ooohh!" replied Abby, who was crying now too. "We don't want you to leave!"

Wanda groaned.

"I'll wait in the truck. Suck it up and say your so longs, kid. You got a plane to catch."

Fred didn't know what to do, so he started bouncing up and down like he was on pogo stick, which instantly turned my tears into sobbing laughter.

"You are SO weird, Fred," I managed to say.

He stopped bouncing and ruffled my Boris Horace hair.

"See you in December, Emma *Freak*?"

I wiped my eyes.

"Really? Will you visit?"

"Ma and Pa thought it was a splendid idea—so warn everyone in Homeport!"

I turned to Abby.

"Can you come too?"

"I doubt we have the extra money for that," she replied.

"Money?" said Fred. "Never let money control your life! We'll figure it out between now and then."

"Okay," said Abby. "I'll try!"

Wanda tapped the horn and hung her head out the window.

"You want to stay here until next year's reunion? 'Cause I got cows to milk!"

The ride home wasn't what I expected, but I should have known. We couldn't talk at all because Wanda had the radio blaring and the windows halfway down. Not to mention, the roar of the old engine was deafening all by itself.

Besides, now I didn't feel like talking. I had such a lump in my throat.

By the time we turned off at the Gas 'n' Gulp, the same one we had stopped at on the way up, I was feeling a little better. And I figured now would be my best chance to ask questions. But as soon as the engine was off, Wanda practically jumped out of the truck to fill it up. I got out on my side and slowly moved to the front of the hood.

"Wanda?" I began. "Can I ask you a couple of things?"

She paused and stared at me. Then she looked at her watch.

"We've made good time," she said. "Let's go in and grab a quick bite."

I needed to use the restroom, so I told Wanda I'd meet her at the booth and to please order me a grilled cheese with tomatoes, bacon, lots of pepper and mayo.

"That's quite a sandwich, kid," she replied.

I smiled. "I know."

Washing my hands, I thought about how to begin this conversation. Wanda wasn't the easiest person in the world to talk to. It was possible, she wouldn't even admit to being my father's sister. And she seemed to only speak in riddles.

As I walked across the restaurant, I was surprised to see her sitting with someone at our table. My heart dropped. She must have run into a friend or another farmer. Now we'd never get a chance to talk.

But as soon as Wanda spotted me, she stood up and pointed in my direction. A thin, bald man slid out of the booth and turned around.

It took me a second to place him, but there was no doubt about it. It was that man from the store. The one who wore dark suits—he was wearing one now—and who had stopped in twice without saying anything. It was pretty bizarre seeing him outside the bead shop in a completely different state. *Was he following me?* Like some sort of detective or spy?

He grinned nervously.

"Um," I hesitated, "aren't you from Homeport?"

"Emma," said Wanda. "I thought you'd like to meet your father, Walter."

Huh?? Now I was totally confused. And more than a little creeped out.

"My *what?*"

I couldn't believe this was happening. I had always expected some incredible moment, meeting my long lost father for the very first time. But definitely not this guy. And definitely not *here* at the Gas 'n' Gulp.

I stared at him. And then I stared at Wanda. And I realized they both had all the classic *Frecky* physical traits. And so did I. And the three of us looked entirely related.

I think I moaned kinda loudly. I actually felt sick.

"Need the washroom again?" asked Wanda.

"No," I answered, rubbing my forehead. "But I'm not too hungry anymore."

"Please," said Walter, "let's all sit and get to know one another a little."

So I slid in next to Wanda, who handed me a glass of ice water, and I listened to my story...and how it all began.

TWENTY - NINE

"Happy travels, kid," said Wanda, as she handed me off to the airline people with all my papers.

We had just made the flight in time. But it would have been worth missing it. Those forty-five minutes with Walter had answered about twelve years' worth of wondering.

It turned out when Walter and Wanda were teenagers living in New Thule, their parents died after their station wagon was sucked up by a tornado in a movie theater parking lot and dropped in a fountain across the street. To make matters worse, Wanda and Walter were forced to live with Aunt Pat as she was listed as every *Frecky* minor's legal guardian.

Aunt Pat was still young herself, but already the boss of everybody. And living with her was far more annoying than just being related. She tracked Wanda's and Walter's every move.

So the day after she turned sixteen, Wanda quit school and left town without a word, just a note asking them not to look for her. As a result, Aunt Pat told Walter that if he pulled any stunts like his sister, he could forget about college tuition or his Boris Horace inheritance. Walter knew an education was his ticket out of New Thule, so he stuck out all four years at Marquette University making Aunt Pat very happy.

What didn't make her happy was the news, a couple years later, that he was dating Donatella, a pasta queen/palm reader whom he'd met on a weekend trip to Boston. Walter was (somehow) smitten with Donatella's free-spirited personality and, at the same time, more than ready to abandon Aunt Pat and the rest of the *Frecky* clan. He had been all too aware of the family expectations and Pat's manipulating ways. So he married my mother, his exact opposite, after knowing her for only one month, against everyone's wishes. Wanda had quit the cruise ship life by then and stood as their only witness at the wedding. And no surprise, Walter (like Wanda) was promptly cut out of the family *and* the will.

"If you sacrificed everything to marry Donatella," I asked Walter, as our waitress served three slices of apple pie, "then why did you leave her?"

"Leave? I didn't leave her," he replied, sounding surprised. "Donatella chased me out of the apartment with a steaming hot pasta fork."

Wanda chuckled a tiny bit, then caught herself and coughed.

"What was she so mad about?" I needed to know.

Walter pushed against the back of the booth and replied, "Who knows? Something I did or said or didn't do or didn't say. But honestly, I think she just grew bored of me. I'm not the most exciting guy in the world."

I'm not exciting either, I thought to myself. But you couldn't get rid of your only daughter. You could only ignore her.

"Did you get married again?"

"No, I didn't," he replied. "Donatella was it for me."

I had no idea. But then again, no one in my family ever told me anything. Everything I knew had been based on assumptions and really bad guesses.

"I hadn't been back to Homeport in more than ten years," explained Walter. "Last month I was on a business trip in the area, so I decided to drop by the store a couple of times hoping to bump into Donatella. But then, when I overheard you telling that gentleman you were her daughter," he said shaking his head, "I was thrown for a loop! Clearly, we were related."

We smiled weakly at each other.

"Well, I was plain furious," he mumbled.

I didn't know what to say except, "I spend a lot of my time mad at Donatella too if it helps any."

That made all three of us crack up.

"Amazing," said Walter. "You laugh exactly like your mother, Emma."

"Really?"

"If I had my eyes closed," he said, "I wouldn't be able to tell the difference."

Wow, I thought to myself, when did that happen?

"So how did I get invited to the reunion?" I asked.

Walter looked down at his half-eaten pie and pushed it around the plate. "I took a chance and wrote Aunt Pat. I thought she'd do the right thing."

I thought about that for a few seconds. "In a way, I guess she did."

At that point, Wanda noticed it was late and we had to get to the airport, but there was so much more to talk about. Walter and I exchanged e-mail addresses, and he asked if I would fly out to visit him in Ohio someday. Without hesitation, I agreed.

I had to ask him one last thing before we left. "Can you please tell me why Donatella mispronounces our last name?"

"To tell you the truth, she doesn't. *Freak* is the correct pronunciation," he said, then pointed north. "They're the ones who pretend it's something else."

OF COURSE, no one was at the Boston airport to meet me. What was I expecting? Donatella would always be Donatella. I had to go through the whole "missing guardian" process one more time. And to top it off, clicky heels Dee-Dee was assigned to me again.

"Hon, your parents have got to get their act together!" she said at full volume as we made our way over to the information desk.

I sighed. "You're telling me."

It turned out my mother had a client scheduled, so she had signed up for one of those airport van drivers to pick me up. Only he had written instructions to pick up an 'Emily Frick.' Luckily, he had the correct address, and Dee-Dee was willing to swear on her career that I was who I claimed to be, so the airport people allowed me to go.

The driver didn't say a word and seemed to be in a terrible hurry, which was fine because I was fully talked out. My brain was still spinning from lunch with Wanda and Walter back at the Gas 'n' Gulp. There was so much to think about.

Dusk had fallen, and the whole world appeared to be glowing. Normally I would have been dreading a return to my pathetic lack of social life and dreary existence, but something deep down inside of me had truly changed. It felt like I had been away three months instead of just three days. And all at once, I couldn't wait to get going with my life.

The driver practically threw my sleeping bag and backpack on the sidewalk in front of the store and sped away like he was off to pick up the emperor of Japan. I stood at the intersection of Harbor Street and Driftwood Lane and noticed how calm it was. No wind. I gazed up at the glittering evening sky. And right away I saw it, the North Star, and I waved.

The shop was locked up and dark except for a small lamp Donatella never turns off. Other than the chain of bells, which jangled as I swung open the door, the building was silent. I poked around the store and dug my hands into several piles of beads, letting them run like streams of water through my fingers. Everything smelled wonderfully familiar.

"Hello?" I called out as I climbed the narrow staircase.

I was surprised to find the small hallway pitch-black and the top door locked too. Again, it felt as if I had been away a very long time and Donatella, Nonno, and Eggplant had packed up and moved while I was gone. I fumbled around with my keys trying to find the keyhole when suddenly someone yanked the door open. Then all the lights flashed on.

"SURPRISE!"

Penelope stood at the doorway, her arms stretched wide open ready for one of her special hugs.

I couldn't believe it. A bunch of people were all cheering loudly and clapping. For me! Donatella, Nonna and Eggplant (in their brown plaid recliner), Stevie, that teacher guy named Gordon, and all eight kids from the library were there. Even my mother's icky friend, Kevin! Streamers and balloons drifted near the ceiling, and the kitchen table was filled with Italian food and drinks.

The old Emma wanted to panic and bolt down the stairs . . . but the new Emma wouldn't let her.

"Thank you!" I said and then laughed. "But what did I do exactly?"

That made the rest of them laugh.

Donatella rushed over and gave my cheeks a hard squeeze.

"It's a *Welcome Home* party, silly! Don't you love it?"

"It was my idea, of course!" hollered Penelope, still clinging to my waist.

"Hey!" Kevin hollered. "'Tella here cooked all weekend!"

Penelope stood on her tiptoes and giggled in my ear.

"Looks like *'Tella's* tofu burgers were too hard for Kevin to resist."

Ugh. I guess some things would never change.

Nonno shifted Eggplant in his lap and asked in his raspy voice, "Where you go, Emma-roni?"

"Hmm, good question, Nonno," I replied and looked over at Stevie. "I guess to the stars and back."

"That good place!"

Everyone laughed again, but Stevie just smiled.

"Emma," she said, "This is also a *Welcome* party."

I was confused. "Welcome to what?"

"Your new school!" said Gordon. "You'll be joining us in the fall. That is, if you think it's a good idea."

I glanced around at the eight kids and noticed Jared, the friendly boy who had talked to Penelope and me in the library.

"You're a real school?" I managed to say, then felt myself blushing.

"It's the special program Ms. Fiddle chose for you," explained Stevie, "for gifted and talented students."

"Ms. Fiddle chose that?"

"Of course she did, 'cause that's what you are, Emma!" cried out Penelope. "Gifted *and* talented!"

That comment set off another round of cheers.

"And I have to say," said Penelope, "my gold mojo bead worked double time . . . 'cause man, you look *gooooood*!"

Life drastically improved for me. It wasn't only due to my new school program, although that was a thousand times better than anything I had ever done in my whole life. And I automatically acquired eight new cool friends. But more important, I had definitely found my *joylah*, my groove zone, my smooth place back in the track. And I was sticking with it forever.

But I think the very best thing that happened that summer occurred in the last week of August when Penelope returned from her annual surprise vacation with the Gray Moms. In past years, they had visited Brazil, the Grand Canyon, and Sri Lanka, to name a few super incredible locations. But this year was different. The surprise trip for Penelope's double-digit tenth birthday was a journey back to Liberia. And she got to meet a whole bunch of her relatives . . . including a very special one.

I was in the back storage room, counting out a shipment of Navajo turquoise beads that had just arrived.

I was thinking about a design to make matching bracelets for Abby and me when the phone rang.

"Emma, I'm home!" Penelope's voice squealed through the receiver. "You gotta come over! Now!"

"Wait! Where did you go this year?"

"I'll tell you when I see you! Meet me on my front porch!"

I hung the "Be Right Back" sign on the door handle and raced across the street. I was so happy Penelope was finally back and couldn't wait to hear all about her latest adventure. Now that I had traveled all the way to Wisconsin by myself, I was anxious to take another trip.

But as I got closer to her front steps, I stopped. Penelope was strangely slumped in one of the wicker rocking chairs with a pile of blankets covering her lap, like she was sick or something.

"Careful," she whispered as I rushed up the stairs.

"What's the matter?" I gasped. "Are you okay?"

All at once, Penelope's lips stretched into an enormous grin as she tilted the pile of blankets toward me. I tiptoed over and saw a face. The sweetest little sleeping face I had ever seen in my whole life.

"This is my *sister*!" she whispered as loudly as she could. "We adopted her in Liberia."

I drifted down to the floor.

"Oh. Wow."

I think I stared in awe at the beautiful baby for a least a full minute before I asked, "What's her name?"

"Well, the Gray Moms named her Winifred, after Katherine's mother, since I'm named after Cynthia's mother. But they let *me* pick her middle name."

"So what did you pick?"

"Emma," she beamed. "Because that's the very best name I know."

How to Find Your Joylah

1. Try new things
2. Be open to new friends
3. Visit new places
4. Listen to new ideas
5. Remember each day is a new day
6. *And it's really no big deal if beads get mixed up every once in a while.*

Acknowledgments

This story journeyed down various roads with guidance and support from a few wonderful people. I could not have completed the trip without my first reader, friend, and agent, Susan Cohen. Also, many thanks to my patient and talented editor, Andrew Karre. And finally, boundless gratitude belongs to my husband, Erik Eames, for giving me the writer's life.